MYSTERY AT THE
WORLD'S EDGE

a&b

MYSTERY AT THE WORLD'S EDGE

Alanna Knight

Allison & Busby Limited
11 Wardour Mews
London W1F 8AN
allisonandbusby.com

First published in Great Britain by Allison & Busby in 2021.

Copyright © 2021 by ALANNA KNIGHT

A CIP catalogue record for this book is available from
the British Library.

First Edition

ISBN 978-0-7490-2765-0

Typeset in 11.5/16.5 pt Sabon LT Pro by
Allison & Busby Ltd.

Printed and bound by
CPI Group (UK) Ltd, Croydon, CR0 4YY

PROLOGUE

In the beginning of time, when the Master Builder had come to the end of his labours of creating the world, he found he had a few fragments of earth still clinging to his hands. He looked down upon the Seven Seas he had just created; then, brushing his fingers lightly together, he sprinkled the fragments through the translucent air so that they fell into the waters of a northern sea. We know them today as Orkney and Shetland; a galaxy of precious stones of rare beauty, as various in their size and outlines as they are in tone and hue.

CHAPTER ONE

CHAPTER ONE

'No! No!' His arm was painful, in the grip of something large and hairy.

A weird monster.

Tam Eildor closed his eyes hastily. Apart from the sore arm he must be dreaming. This was a nightmare. Sound, sea nearby. Water, oceans of it, great lapping waves. Seabirds everywhere, wheeling in the sky above with their screeches.

Other screeches, no, screams. Human screams.

Where was he? This bleak, inhospitable land. He knew then. A dreadful mistake had been made; the time machine had developed a digital error. He had to get back again and in that last hope of survival, he reached for the panic button on his wrist.

It was covered by a mouth, the mouth of a huge animal. He was not only in the wrong time, he was to be eaten by a sea monster. This was his last travel through time. Had he belonged to the world long lost he would have believed in prayers, God the Master Builder. His instinct was still for survival as he struggled against dying, but he found it painless. He was not being eaten, at least not yet, but being dragged along the shoreline by an overgrown wolf with a dog-like head.

Now his first nervous thought was that he had fallen into some prehistoric period and that such creatures were now extinct in his own time. He opened his eyes again with difficulty, dreading dinosaurs, and found himself the target of two quite extraordinary humanoids. Certainly not from his own time. This must be the Dark Ages, centuries away from the Victorian Edinburgh he had planned to visit.

About a yard distant and looking more predatory than the wolf-dog was the ugliest woman he had ever set eyes on. She was tiny, just as tall as the animal and covered with black hair, most of it on her head. Her huge feet at the end of her short legs were out of all proportion.

'Zor! Leave him!' The command belonged to an old man with a white beard, the longest Tam had ever seen.

The wolf-dog had now released his arm and was being restrained from licking his face. That was what had wakened him lying on a stony beach. He tried to rise, push the animal aside. Was this a preliminary sniff, a prelude to its intended lunch? But almost reproachfully its regard was not predatory. Its head on its side it had a friendly, oddly human expression identical to the man who supported him, an illustration escaped from a fairy tale about an ancient wizard.

Tam made a determined effort and sat up, eager hands assisting him.

'We tried to take that thing off your neck,' said the woman.

'We thought you'd be strangled,' added the man.

Thankful for words he could understand, Tam touched the charm stone, passport to all that connected him with his own world.

'We couldna move it.'

Nothing on this earth at this time would do so and he silently thanked the Master Builder, the scientific creator, for the progress discovered after Planet Earth's partial collapse in the twenty-second century. Drowned by melting ice caps in the climate change unheeded by nations for over a hundred years and overpopulated, its resources for survival, for crops growing each year, failed and it had never recovered. That was three hundred years ago before the escape to Planet B and the emergence of a new scientific civilisation with the subsequent discovery of travel through time as well as space that had proved a boon to those interested in ancient history.

For scholars like himself it provided a delightful chance to explore lost worlds and the continued progress of scientific experiments. And for those keen to travel, the inconvenience of grappling with foreign languages had been surpassed by the discovery of a universal automatic understanding.

Tam Eildor particularly enjoyed criminology and reading about true crimes. He was rather proud that he shared an interest in unsolved mysteries with detectives, both fictional and real, in the nineteenth and twentieth centuries. Sherlock Holmes was of special interest as were many other crime writers' detectives. Tam felt an affinity with those who, like himself, claimed Scottish descent from the ancient world and enjoyed dabbling in the Victorian era.

He had dialled 1857, his chosen year for this adventure, with his particular interest in the sensational trial of Madeleine Smith. She was believed to have murdered her lover, a Frenchman and socially far beneath her. She had escaped hanging by the Scottish 'not proven' verdict, after raising considerable doubts. Heads were shaken, whispers remained that the jury had been influenced by the fact that this was a beautiful twenty-two-year-old, her wealthy family well-connected and high in Glasgow society.

Tam was fascinated and a little in love with the notorious murderess. He had decided he would like to meet Madeleine Smith and investigate for himself, on the reported evidence given in the old documents, whether she was innocent or a skilful killer.

He groaned. What a disaster that impulse had been. By no stretch of the imagination could this bleak, cold seashore with these two humanoids and their dog-like companion be the place of a civilised assignation.

'Where am I, and what year is this?'

Looks were exchanged by the weird pair. The question

obviously amused them, and they chose to ignore it. Perhaps they thought he had temporarily lost his wits.

The old man said politely, 'You would have been carried out to the sea by the ebb tide had Zor not seized you.'

Tam looked at the wolf-dog, who regarded him fixedly and nodded, as if rather proud of his efforts.

'You would have drowned,' the man continued. 'Are you hurt?' he added anxiously. 'Perhaps you hit your head when you fell.'

'Did I? What is this place?' Tam asked, in the hope that he was in England or Scotland and not in some foreign land.

The man stroked his long white beard and said, 'Orkney, young sir. Surely you know the date, the summer of 1587.' He laughed at the question which seemed absurd and asked, 'And who might you be?'

'Tam Eildor. And you are?'

'I am Doctor Erasmus Linmer,' the wizard-like man bowed and, pointing to the tiny woman, said, 'This is Baubie Finn, a skilful islander. We will take good care of you.'

'1587, did you say?' Tam repeated, wondering if his hearing had been affected by the fall and rapidly sorting through disorganised thoughts and somewhat limited observation.

By all accounts and the efficiency of the time machine's workings, he should be in one of those splendid Georgian houses in Edinburgh's New Town enjoying a glass of excellent brandy or in Glasgow with Madeleine Smith and a glass of excellent wine. On second thoughts, maybe wine would be inadvisable, but anything remotely linked to that lost civilised society and popular, like a cup of tea, would be preferable to lying on a stony beach in Orkney, in damp clothes.

He groaned again, his mind managing a quick calculation.

1587. The year before the Spanish Armada.

He made an effort to get to his feet, hampered by the huge wolf-dog that hovered over him in a determined fashion. His yelp of surprise as he took in his surroundings could have issued from the animal itself.

'It can't be 1587. Are you sure?'

Three heads, including wolf-dog Zor, nodded solemnly.

Tam thought quickly. 'Orkney. That would be in the reign of Earl Robert Stewart?'

There were more solemn and now distressed noddings and sighings.

Tam straightened his shoulders and gazed around helplessly, rubbing his sore arm, thankful that Zor had not taken a bite on the chip he wore on his left wrist. It was bruised but not broken; the panic button remained intact.

And now he knew what had happened. That damned time mechanism, usually so reliable, had misplaced the digits: 1857, the year he had dialled, had become 1587.

That was unheard of. Had the fault been his own? They would certainly claim so. They would say he had been careless. There would be witnesses that on the night before his booked-in departure, a little overindulgence in wine and sociability, and by careless fingering, the digits of the two dates had been reversed.

He swore silently. That was bad enough, but worst of all he had landed in the wrong reign. Another quick calculation. James the Sixth would now be on the Scottish throne, impatiently biding his time for the ailing Queen Elizabeth of England to die, when he would become James I of England.

He knew his history and Earl Robert Stewart was the illegitimate half-brother of Mary, Queen of Scots, who had given him Orkney and a tyrannous reign that Tam had not the slightest desire to experience. It was a mysterious land to be avoided, feared by long-ago mariners as 'one of the islands at the world's edge'.

'I heard cries, people screaming. Was there some er . . . disturbance? I thought I was on a battlefield.' As he said the words, an additional, graver reason for discomfort presented itself: the Orcadians were known, if not as cannibals, than most certainly as wreckers, their very existence dependent on luring ships ashore, stripping them of all cargo and grimly leaving no survivors, with more than enough starving men, women and bairns of their own to feed and clothe.

The old man shook his head. 'Not a battlefield. That was a wreck.' His frown into the middle distance confirmed Tam's suspicions. 'Further down the coast.'

'Did the passengers survive?'

Uncomfortable looks were exchanged between the man and woman, so Tam guessed what the answer would be.

The old man said hastily: 'It was too far off for us to be certain. Nothing to do with us.'

'The Earl—' the woman began and received a gentle warning nudge.

But Tam was getting his bearings. In Orkney at that time wreckers took no prisoners.

The grim picture that was emerging offered scant consolation. James the Sixth was King of Scotland and, on a previous time quest, in 1567, he had encountered the then unborn baby James's mother, Mary, Queen of Scots, in the mysterious affair at Kirk O'Field in Edinburgh and the murder of her dreadful husband Lord Darnley.

He groaned as he recalled time travelling again in 1600. He had the misfortune to become one of the young king's amorous pursuits, as James determinedly eliminated all those connected with the truth of the Gowrie Conspiracy and the sinister matter of who had forged many of the Casket Letters that proved to be Mary's death sentence, in 1587 of this very year.

Tam shuddered. He had had more than enough of this particular period of history.

He looked round desperately. A dreadful mistake had been made. He had to get back to his own time again and, in that last hope of survival, he reached for the panic button at his wrist. If he didn't escape, he was marked down as lunch for the monster Zor and cannibals too, for that was what the wreckers probably were.

But this was his last travel through time.

Both Zor and the humans were eyeing him sternly, and it occurred to him as none made a predatory move that they were as startled by his appearance as he was

14

by theirs.

He tried a friendly, hopeful smile.

The woman responded by asking him a question requiring an answer, but at that moment her accent was beyond him.

She shook her head, oddly echoed by Zor.

He had an idea: the animal was one of those robotic creatures used in past centuries. But then he remembered the one who pulled him out of the sea had distinct breath, warm and smelly, as any of those kept as pets where he came from.

'You have come a long way,' said the old man. 'You must be tired and should rest a while.' Pointing to what looked like a deep cave at the headland, he continued, 'Come, young sir, and Baubie will give you some of her excellent soup and a bed for the night.'

Tam stood up and found that he was shaken but unhurt, apart from a bruised arm, thanks to the efforts of his rescuer's jaws. His clothes had dried remarkably quickly and there in the sky above, the sun was a comforting reminder of his own planet, shining benignly down as he followed the trio across the wind-beaten, uninhabited beach towards the base of a steep cliff where, above the rocky shore, the mouth of a dark, forbidding cave yawned.

He trembled at the thought of going inside.

Should he make a run for it?

CHAPTER TWO

Where to run to? That was the question. While he was trapped by this weird couple, it was difficult to run anywhere. The woman, who was remarkably strong considering her size, had his arm firmly in her grip. It was as though she could snap it off as easily as a butterfly wing, without the slightest difficulty or emotion if occasion demanded. He was also supported, or rather hustled along towards the cave, on his other side by the old man, his strong arms undiminished by age.

Tam sighed, suddenly glad of their help. His legs felt weak, and he had never felt this tired and hungry before. Time travel had taken a lot out of him, and that was a new experience.

As the cave loomed nearer, it looked singularly barbaric and primitive. Tam wanted to sit down on the boulder outside, gather his scattered wits and consider what to do next.

Tam Eildor was no coward and enjoyed adventures in time, but only those with a guaranteed happy ending. He was fully aware of the dangers looming ahead with this particular era of the sixteenth century and regrettably accepted the truth that he was not the stuff that heroes are made of.

There seemed to be no escape. He was being dragged inside, which suggested that he was a prisoner, although his captors murmured encouragingly and the cave's interior was surprisingly large and airy, more like a civilised house cut into a cliffside.

The woman, Baubie, beckoned him to a seat. She smiled at him and suddenly he was pleased and reassured by his surroundings. He started to accept that his companions' intentions were well-meaning and they meant him no harm.

The huge Zor had returned, giving Tam a mite of uneasiness as it continued to regard him with the inscrutable intensity of a diner considering an interesting menu. As significant looks were exchanged between the wolf-dog and the old man, Tam's fears returned and for one dreadful moment he believed these islanders were cannibals after all.

However, as he tried to dismiss his fearful anxiety that he had fallen among flesh-eaters, the woman went briskly to a stove and, after a noisy ritual of stirring liquid, produced a bowl of something which she handed to Tam. He was hungry and to his astonishment found himself enjoying a large bowl of soup and a chunk of coarse bread.

The darkness of the cave no longer overwhelmed him. With sconces on the walls, it was lighter inside than he had expected, and somehow felt warm and safe. Suddenly aware that the second bowl of soup had made him thirsty, he gulped down the contents of the goblet Baubie Finn held out.

Thanking her, he closed his eyes briefly.

The doctor watched Tam peacefully sleeping thanks to his overindulgence with one of Baubie's liquid restoratives. Linmer realised gloomily that he needed, and with haste, to know more about this intriguing young man who cast no shadow. According to the ancient Greeks, the shadow was the soul and one should avoid looking at one's reflection in water; its absence was an omen of death. If a man dreamt of seeing himself so mirrored, the water spirits – in the case of Orkney, selkies – would drag his reflection underwater, leaving him to perish soulless.

Eye contact was also to be avoided. Narrowly regarding Tam, Linmer recalled that when they had met, the young man's eyes had reminded him less of other humans' and more of Zor's, whose existence on this peninsula had never been explained, nor could it be, since the dog lacked a human voice to further expand on the matter.

Linmer frowned. He did not like mysteries and both creatures had strangely luminous eyes. He considered how they were going to deal with Tam and keep him out of Earl Robert Stewart's way. No one was safe from the Earl, especially newcomers, for that wily man had eyes and spies everywhere. Many who had landed unannounced found their way blocked by an executioner's sword without time or hope of explaining, or giving a valid reason for their arrival.

Although Tam slept without dreaming, he thought he awoke and Baubie Finn was watching over him, except that she was no longer a wizened woman but a very beautiful girl. How extraordinary.

As for Baubie Finn, she sighed. Here was the handsomest man she had ever seen, even better than her husband, Halcro, who all the girls in Orkney had chased once long ago. She enjoyed just looking at this Tam Eildor. He seemed so young and vulnerable.

Halcro had arrived home from fishing and joined the watchers over the sleeping man. He wanted something to eat, only vaguely interested in the scene before him and the lengthy explanations regarding a young man who had just dropped in from the skies. Long used to arriving home to unusual situations or visitors with explanations he could not and did not wish to comprehend, he asked no questions. He loved a peaceful home life and Baubie's excellent cooking above all things, was used to being ignored and happy to remain so.

The next thing Tam knew, he was waking up with the sun shining in through the cave mouth and being told by Doctor Linmer that he had slept for twenty-four hours. When Tam was introduced to Halcro and learnt that Baubie was his wife, he could hardly credit that any normal man could have married her, before he succumbed to sleep once more. But Halcro could have told him something about that.

Baubie Finn was second only in power to the Earl himself, the most feared as well as the most sought-after woman on the island. To the less romantically inclined she was also the ugliest woman most of them had ever seen.

Her black and luxuriant hair, which many women would have envied as a crowning glory, grew low on her forehead to well below her non-existent waist. It refused to be confined to her head and wandered to less attractive regions of her face, with its large nose and fearsome squint, while huge hands and feet would have been excessive in persons thrice her height.

The Orcadians had a bad reputation as wreckers and Baubie had stumbled on a particularly potent spell for luring distressed ships to the rocks, used sparingly and only in desperate times, for she was a healer, not a destroyer. A dark wooden barrel on her kitchen shelf in the cave contained a yellowish liquid, nauseous to smell and loathsome to taste, dispensed in tiny bottles hastily corked, the main ingredients salt, asafoetida and other pungent herbs to purge the bowels and purify the blood. A sweeter medicine would have been equally effective, but Baubie pandered to her customers' belief: the nastier the taste the speedier the cure.

No trouble was too great for Baubie. She would patiently search out seven mothers whose firstborn were sons, to provide milk for a sick child at the gates of death. She wove black underwear for rheumatism sufferers and nursed a highly private recipe for locating buried treasure – alas, still unfulfilled.

Love thy neighbour might have been written especially for her, since she cherished the islanders fiercely, but shipwrecked foreign mariners fell into another category. She regarded their violent deaths with as little emotion as the annual seal cull or the occasional stranded whale. Foreigners and their welfare were God's business, not hers. Compassion for the island only extended to its birds and animals who would come right up to her large feet and sit waiting patiently for titbits.

Halcro viewed Baubie's activities with apprehension and trembled at the power wielded by his tiny wife. One never knew what she might conjure up. He had in his time produced for her pot many revolting but not unusual specimens. For her cures the excreta of both animal and human were in constant demand: fresh pig dung for nose bleeds, cow dung poultices for bruised limbs, sweetened urine for jaundice and milk in which sheep's droppings had been boiled for smallpox. Besides mice roasted for whooping cough and snails dissolved in vinegar for rickets, there were many others, the memory of which Halcro preferred not to dwell upon.

Baubie could with considerable ease change into a shrew when thwarted, a transformation he did not care to witness. By giving her her own way, life was not only harmonious but occasionally even sweet. She was rare company and could make him laugh. After some of her herbal remedies she was no longer old and ugly as she

21

danced towards him, but the slim and beautiful girl he had wooed and won long ago.

Then there was the business of the Book of Black Arts, the source of some of her favourite recipes. He had never known a moment's peace while it was under their roof. This manual of magic printed in white characters on black paper gave to its owner unlimited power. However, as with all the Devil's gifts, there was a snag. This particular snag was that the book could only be resold for a smaller coin than it was paid for. Baubie, young and inexperienced at the time, had thought that the man at the Kirkwall Fair was giving her a great bargain until she knew the ultimate price.

However, recently, the rapacious Earl Robert had eagerly accepted it as a gift. Halcro shuddered, still remembering its opening page: 'Cursed be he that peruseth me'. He wondered if the greedy Earl realised the potential destruction he had in his possession, since Baubie had already placed him under St Ringan's Curse, used only by those who had suffered intolerable wrongs without other means of punishing their oppressors.

Baubie felt the Earl and his sons richly deserved the fate St Ringan offered: a family cursed to the second and third generation – at which juncture they died out.

CHAPTER THREE

Tam was horrified to find, on next opening his eyes and blinking rapidly, that he was not back in his own time, in the world centuries ahead of these primitive humans. Voices surrounded him and he sat up confused as Linmer and Baubie started to ask him questions without waiting for sensible answers, if such were even possible. At last, the woman paused for breath and, seizing opportunity, the old man said:

'I am glad you are alive, young man, and have taken no ill from your dramatic arrival. When I saw you suddenly appear, descending from the sky, I thought my mind was playing tricks and this was the Second Coming we had been told to daily expect from the Bible.' He regarded Tam sternly. 'You don't look like Jesus Christ, however, not as I have imagined him.' Sounding disappointed he added, 'What brings you to the islands at the world's end?'

Tam groaned and, for the first time, he took an interest in what he was wearing. No one had removed his clothes as he slept: a wide-sleeved white shirt, full thigh boots and tight breeches. Surely a little updated for Orkney and these surroundings as he considered the area outside the cave where he had landed.

His audience were waiting. 'My name is Tam Eildor,' he announced and inclined his head.

Linmer smiled knowingly, then frowned and gave a clever chuckle. 'An anagram. So, you are a time lord, are you? At least that explains how you came to be travelling through space. For a moment I was quite alarmed. Unprepared, you know.' He gave Tam a hard look and sighed.

Watching the man as he slept, Linmer had made other interesting observations besides the fact that he cast no shadow. His clothes were made of some unknown material, an immaculate white shirt that didn't show creases where he'd slept, nor any evidence of being dragged across the shore by Zor, but most of all how after two days on the island this young man showed no signs of needing a shave. There was no trace of beard, his face still quite smooth, although he was to all appearances a perfectly normal fellow in his mid-thirties.

Tam was watching the doctor, now guessing that Linmer was most probably a fellow time traveller who had gone off-course and been forced to remain in the time he had chosen. This conclusion filled Tam with horror as Linmer went on: 'This is a pleasant surprise, young sir. You are the first time lord I have ever met. What brought you to Orkney at this dire period of our history?'

And here at last was an intelligent being, someone he could get information from. 'It's a mistake, I'm afraid. I was hoping for – for a later date in Edinburgh—,' he added, knowing it was unlikely that Linmer would know about the sensational trial of Madeleine Smith centuries on.

He realised the urgency the days he had lost and the danger that he was in. He had better get on with it, complete his visit to this lacklustre beach as soon as possible. It was not possible to switch missions or places. Much as he would have relished heading on to Edinburgh, it would mean abandoning this particular mission and returning to the year 2300 to start over again. What a nuisance. But first, he had better find his exact location. He could not afford any more digital errors with the time machine. 'Where am I, er, exactly?' Tam asked.

'Exactly is hard to say. You are on one of the more obscure of our tiny peninsulas, the broch, only accessible to Kirkwall at low tide. This is the home of Lady Marie Hepburn. Come with me.'

Tam followed him out of the cave and they walked a short distance uphill, where Linmer pointed to a large, ungainly building and said, 'That is a broch, one of our prehistoric ruins. Some have identified it as Neolithic for convenience, but its exact history is unknown. No one can say exactly, merely offer theories about when or who had built it. The archaeologists gave up long ago.'

'Someone actually lives in it?' Tam asked in amazement.

'Indeed, as I told you. The Earl's ward, Lady Marie Hepburn, daughter of Lord Bothwell and Mary, Queen of Scots.'

Tam seemed to remembered that Mary had been executed in February 1587 by her cousin, Queen Elizabeth, as Linmer continued bitterly,

'She is more prisoner than ward, I fear, locked away in this cold place since the Earl rescued her and took her captive. The ship she believed was taking her to her father was taken by wreckers.' He shook his head. 'She was eight years old at the time and has lived in captivity for the last twelve years. The Earl, we understand, has plans to marry her off to one of his sons, seeing the possibly of a path to the throne of Scotland by his own blood.'

Even at that distance and without a meeting, Tam felt a surge of indignation for a young woman kept in such dreary seclusion.

'Why didn't the Earl keep her in his castle in Kirkwall?'

Linmer laughed. 'You might well ask, but you wouldn't need to if you knew his six sons. She had to be kept safe from them. He has his heir, Patrick, in mind, but all of them are notorious for their dealings with the young women there. They will not take no for an answer. It is whispered they have peopled half the island.' He frowned sadly. 'So, it was more for her own safety than a tender-hearted gesture. However, she is under the care and protection of Baubie Finn, a formidable target for any intruder—'

Linmer stopped suddenly. 'Listen!'

Tam had also heard the sound of approaching horses.

'That is the Earl's men come to inspect what was left of the wreck before it is too late,' Linmer said urgently. 'Remember the noise you heard when you arrived, young sir, a boat from Edinburgh washed ashore. No accident,' he added wryly. 'Wrecking is an occupation and our ministers are known to pray for one when times are hard. The islanders are not to be blamed, for they are starving thanks to the Earl and they take no prisoners,' he added grimly. 'They cannot afford to feed their own people so you were lucky not to fall into their hands. It was the wreck that alerted me or I would not have seen you descend from the skies, young man.'

He paused and took Tam's arm. 'But you are no longer safe. We must hide you and, all things considered, the broch would be the best place until we decide what to do with you. Poor Marie, she was told to expect a tutor, a Hepburn cousin, arranged by the Earl, of course, for her spiritual well-being.'

He shook his head. 'I regard any such proposition with suspicion, for one learns to always look for a purpose behind any kindly gesture of the Earl. He is a crafty man, though for what purpose this tutor was sent for I can only regard that he was a spy, although the motive, I was given to understand, is that as his alchemist I had enough to deal with.'

Tam smiled. An alchemist. Well, that fitted well enough.

Linmer continued, 'The Earl loves gold and somewhat naively believes blood can be got from a stone. He is sure

27

there is gold in Orkney and that an alchemist should be able to find it. He also pointed out what I already knew that I was not getting older.' Then with a laugh, 'He is not very observant, since I have been this age for longer than I care to remember.'

'When did you arrive?'

Tam was interested and keen to know more, but as they had reached their destination and walked towards the gate of the broch, Zor ran out to greet them.

There was some tail-wagging as if he was pleased to welcome this new visitor, and again its expression was almost human. Tam had never seen an animal behave in such a way and Linmer said, 'Zor lives here with Lady Marie. An excellent guard; no one can get past him. Fortunate that he had come down to the beach when you arrived so unexpectedly.'

'Fortunate indeed,' Tam agreed.

'He's a remarkable creature and has an extra sense of perception and danger – perhaps we all had that at one time – but he knows what is imminent and was aware of the wreck before it happened.'

As Zor led the way like a guide taking visitors through the ancient stone portals, Tam looked around. The broch defied any knowledge he had of prehistoric building. When he said so, Linmer contributed his own theory that the original broch builders were probably missionaries anxious to spread Christianity over as wide an area as possible.

'It most resembles an enormous lighthouse in shape,' Tam observed, pausing to look upwards.

Linmer continued knowledgeably, 'Indeed, it does. You are seeing a fortress surrounded by a stone wall. There was no roof in the original, only a circular penthouse running round the inside,' he added, leading the way.

Following him, Tam saw that it was double-walled and between them a series of stone galleries were linked by a stairway curving upwards towards the top. The flagstone floor of each gallery formed the ceiling of the one below, with daylight provided by small window gaps on the inner wall only.

The effect seemed singularly formidable, too enormous for hospitality, and Tam wondered how it would be possible for comfort surrounded by such a vast area of stone.

Certainly not for a young woman on her own with few servants. Its purpose seemed more barrack-like, with the hint of armed men preparing for battle. When he said so, Linmer replied, 'What purpose the galleries served was perhaps as scaffolding in the original building. That stairway certainly would let defenders climb to the top when it was attacked by invaders. You probably did not have time to notice as we came up from the beach some ruins of crude stone huts that once surrounded it, perhaps used to delay attackers when the broch's owners retired within.'

Tam considered this and said, 'That would certainly have been an advantage as there would have been few weapons in ancient times to make any impression on such thick walls which could not be burnt down.'

Linmer nodded. 'And it would be almost impossible to force an entrance through the narrow doorway.'

From what he had seen so far, Tam was impressed. The broch dwellers had been well equipped to withstand a siege.

Linmer went on, 'Like many buildings of ancient times, this one has a well inside, and provisions could be stored in the stone galleries.'

Looking round, Tam observed that spears could have been thrust down from the galleries above through gaps left between the roofing stones of the passage. While he was still considering their surroundings in awe and amazement, Linmer added thoughtfully, 'I think if Lady Marie agrees, you will be safe here until we decide what is to be done before you encounter Earl Robert.'

Seeing from Tam's doubtful expression that this was not a prospect that pleased him nor was the encounter to be anticipated with any jubilation, Linmer said, 'Lady Marie lives in one part where the ruined galleries have been turned into liveable and even attractive quarters, almost like a small castle..'

He pointed to a stone bench. 'Let us take a seat and wait for her.'

As they talked, Zor had stood alongside them, in an attitude of listening eagerly. It seemed to take a human interest in the conversation, understanding all that was being said, looking from one to the other and occasionally nodding, as if in agreement with the discussion.

A weird creature indeed, Tam decided, and this seemed an opportune moment to discover the rest of Linmer's story of how he came to be in Orkney. As a scholar, he could hardly have chosen this bleak peninsula and when Tam asked him, he shook his head wearily.

'It was so long ago I can barely remember, a survivor before even the disaster that overtook Planet Earth. As a scientist working on time experiments, it seemed that I got trapped and could not get my way back to the place I had left.' He paused. 'The Earl knew nothing of time experiments, but presumed that I was an alchemist and as such welcomed the possibility of finding gold, his favourite pastime.' He smiled wryly. 'How much of the history of Orkney do you know?'

'Not a great deal, but enough not to wish to get stranded here.' Tam shuddered. 'It was not my intention to come here – my intention was to come to mainland Scotland in the nineteenth century.'

Footsteps on the long staircase announced a new arrival. Not Marie, but a servant, who Linmer greeted as Ina. In reply she nodded eagerly, but clearly had no voice.

As she hurried back up the stairs, Linmer explained, 'She can't speak, has no tongue. It was cleft by the Earl's command when she had the temerity to speak ill of the amorous intentions of one of his sons.'

At Tam's shocked exclamation, he sighed bitterly. 'That is one of the lesser punishments, often it is death. So be careful that your comments are never overheard. One criticism or bad word about the Earl's sons could be your last.'

He smiled. 'Lady Marie will be with us in a moment. Ina has just washed her hair and she will see us once it dries.'

That was such a common reason, a ready excuse in days long past for females to make excuses for non-appearance and it made Tam smile.

'She will be with us soon and, alas, I will have to impart the sad news about the death of her expected tutor, Edward Hepburn.' Linmer frowned and, stroking his beard thoughtfully, he regarded Tam. 'But what are we to do with you? Do you want to return to your own time now? No doubt your presence here has been registered. The Earl has spies everywhere and he will have received news of a stranger at the broch. If you wish to quit you must do so now.'

But regardless of the dangers as yet unheralded, Tam was sufficiently intrigued by the strange trio of time lord turned alchemist, the small woman and a dog-like creature with human intelligence, all the ingredients of a Grimm's Fairy Tale, including a princess, the prisoner of a tyrant lord. What a splendid opportunity! Having never pictured himself in the role of a knight errant, there was plenty at this moment to make the time machine's digital error an irresistible challenge.

'I will stay for a while.' Even as he said the words, he thought of the consequences of being taken before the Earl and explaining that he had come from the future. What lay ahead would be complete disbelief and doubtless torture until he could find some acceptable version of the truth. Tam shuddered, but Linmer was watching him, smiling.

'I have just thought of a plan, Tam Eildor, one that will fit you perfectly. Here I was wondering how on earth to fit you in with some creditable story and now I realise that your arrival, your unexpected descent from the sky, could not have come more opportunely. You are sufficiently educated and well-bred to present yourself in the role as Lady Marie's new tutor, her distant uncle from the Bothwells at Crichton Castle. I trust you are a good actor for the part will suit you incredibly well.'

Linmer paused, for even as he said the words, he realised the possibilities of presenting Lady Marie with an unusually attractive young man and the consequences for both of them of a sudden infatuation. He added hastily, 'Think of yourself as Edward Hepburn as soon as you can, God rest his soul.'

He had another reason for passing Tam off successfully as the tutor, a plan for how to smuggle Lady Marie back to Scotland. Each passing day brought her closer to broch marriage to the Earl's disreputable eldest son, Patrick. He had been recently widowed in a childless marriage and his well-earned bad reputation had already labelled him among the islanders as Black Pate, for good reason.

Linmer rubbed his hands in satisfaction as he studied Tam, who could not have been better suited for the deceased tutor's role. He chuckled gleefully. 'An excellent plan, if you agree.'

Ina reappeared on the stairway and indicated to the two men that her mistress was ready and waiting to receive them.

Zor accompanied them as they followed her along a short corridor, where she opened the door into a well-lit room considerably more comfortable than Tam's first expectations. Along with tapestried walls and a rug-covered floor, further adornments included portraits and silver.

Linmer took Tam's arm and as they bowed, then started to walk across to the woman sitting by the window, he whispered, 'First of all you must meet Lady Marie Hepburn and here she is.'

CHAPTER FOUR

Lady Marie stood up at their approach and Tam was immediately aware that she was regarding him intently, her hand on Zor's head. A long, slender hand was all that reminded him of her Stuart connection. There was nothing of her beautiful tall mother in the girl before him. She was completely Bothwell's child, with her short stature and his fox-coloured hair. He guessed already from what Linmer had told him that only her Borderer's toughness had helped her survive twelve years as a prisoner, where a girl more delicately reared would have been destroyed.

Zor had taken his place by her side and was also watching him with the same intensity. On a perch nearby a magpie, its head on one side, viewed this newcomer with the same curiosity and suspicion.

Tam did not care for large wolves or dogs or magpies and felt not only uncomfortable but oddly threatened, as if these odd bodyguards of the princess might at a word descend upon him.

'Caw!' He shuddered as the magpie screeched angrily and fluttered down from its perch to regard Tam, from a point of greater advantage. Extending its wings, it assumed the appearance of a bird of prey.

That Tam was unnerved by this close encounter was evident to Marie, who laughed and said, 'This is Mags, my faithful friend and companion. You have nothing to fear from her. She is very reliable, her only weakness is jewellery. All visitors are inspected carefully and if any are wearing something that sparkles, she will do her best to steal it.'

Linmer shook his head. 'I have seen her at work, but you need not worry, sir.' Turning back to the lady, he began, 'However—' A deep breath signified that he was about to embark on one of his lengthy tales of the shipwreck and, smiling, she interrupted.

'I have already heard from the servants about the wreck.' She held up a dismissive hand. 'You may leave us, good doctor.' She regarded Tam steadily. 'A room has been prepared for you.' She smiled at Zor. 'We will take good care of this gentleman, will we not?'

Zor nodded as if in agreement while Linmer left a little reluctantly, Tam thought, deprived of the rare chance of a dramatic announcement to enliven his isolated existence.

However, as soon as the door closed, Marie indicated two handsome armchairs by a cheery fireside. 'We will be more comfortable there, sir. Even on a sunny day, the rooms become somewhat chilly.'

Bowing, he waited for her to sit down. Instead, she frowned at him for a moment before pointing an accusing finger. 'You are not my Uncle Hepburn.'

Tam's bewildered expression agreed with that denunciation and she smiled. 'I met him when I was a small girl. He was short and bald.' She continued to survey this handsome young man appreciatively, with his tall frame and his thick, black hair. 'So who might you be, sir?'

While Tam was conjuring up a suitable response, she said, 'You are a survivor from the wreck.'

He did not expect to have any more success with Lady Marie than he gloomily anticipated with Earl Robert, but hoped that the torture would not be included, as Marie had sat down and he took the chair opposite. Zor sat in the centre between them and Mags perched on the arm of the chair, both with undiminished eager expressions of suspicion which he found a little unnerving, especially as they seemed not only to take a great interest, but understood every word spoken.

No wonder the princess felt safe with these unusual guards, thought Tam. They made him uneasy, unused to wolves or such large dogs for they were almost extinct in his own time. One wrong move, he thought grimly, and that would be his last. As for the magpie, she had a very cruel beak and would doubtless use it to pluck out eyes if danger threatened her beloved mistress.

Suppressing a shudder, he said, 'My name is Tam Eildor. As you rightly guessed, madam, Dr Linmer rescued me from the wreck. I am a lawyer from Edinburgh.' He did not bother to include some invention about the purpose of this visit to Orkney and hoped she would not ask him before he had time to think of some plausible reason.

Marie nodded. 'A lawyer indeed. Might be useful, might it not?' That was addressed to Zor who also nodded his approval.

Tam sighed. So far, so good, but he was not yet at ease under the watchful gaze of both creatures.

'You are very gracious, my lady,' he said, inclining his head.

She smiled. 'Just Marie, if we are to be better acquainted. I have few friends, small chance to make them. As the good doctor will have told you I have been a prisoner in this wretched place for many years.'

She stifled a sob and Zor immediately moved nearer, his head on her knee, while Mags fluttered her wings and cawed sympathetically.

'My parents, Mary the Queen and Lord Bothwell were married. Poor mother, they parted company – for ever it was to be, though they did not know it at the time. She was rejected by her subjects and imprisoned in Lochleven Castle. There I was born, the survivor of premature twins.' She paused, her sigh reminding Tam of the high mortality rate for even normal royal pregnancies in these long-ago centuries.

'As mother was moved from prison to prison to end her long captivity in February this year' – she paused to stifle a sob and fought back tears, before continuing – 'I was taken care of by Hepburn relatives at their various palaces in the Borders, including Crichton with Uncle Edward, for a while. But for reasons both personal and political, there were conditions I was too young to understand, why a small girl was not welcomed with open arms and a permanent home by cousins and other relatives.

'My stays were of a short duration and my childhood memories sad.' She shivered as she remembered. 'I was always cold and often wakened during the night to be hustled away to yet another castle. I remembered only whispered frantic conversations of danger, sounds of shouting and gunshots.'

What a dreadful childhood, Tam thought as he listened to her. That accounted for the look of steel she had inherited from her father and the lack of ethereal beauty her mother possessed. She needed to be tough and strong to survive and, although attractive, she fitted his initial recognition of a girl more Border-bred than royal Stuart.

'Sometimes I was happy in a sunny castle with pretty gardens for a few days, but these were always plagued by anxious looks and conspiratorial grown-up conversations. I was always conscious that I was different to those other children I played with, but I had no idea then of what they were discussing, nor my value as a pawn in the political chess game.'

She paused to offer Tam a drink of indifferent weak wine from the tray that the silent Ina had laid on the table at her side.

Marie straightened her shoulders and said proudly, 'Yes, I was invaluable in the political game, as the daughter of Mary and Bothwell. I was soon to discover that I was of considerable use to whoever held me with even the vaguest claim to the throne of Scotland. Long queues were already forming over the years.'

Pausing, she smiled sadly. 'By the time I was eight, I learnt that the loyal Hepburns had a plan to take me to join my father, who I had never met. I was pleased. It sounded exciting, hopeful and worthwhile, but the truth was that my presence had become a burden. Too many people wanted to make use of my blood connection to the throne of Scotland.

'I was told my father had escaped and waited for me in Orkney, where he had taken sanctuary after leaving Edinburgh. They had kept the truth from me, that he had been betrayed by all those he believed were his friends. When my father was refused refuge, he fled on to Norway believing that his former betrothed would help him. However, she had been waiting patiently for years for revenge, after his abandonment of her and her son.'

She paused and added, 'The ship I travelled on was seized passing Orkney and spies of the Earl Robert Stewart realised the potential power of this royal captive.' She smiled bitterly, remembering. 'His castle in Kirkwall would have been difficult to keep me a virgin, safe from his scheming sons until I was of a "marriageable prospect". She emphasised the words. 'As you can see, only part of the broch is habitable, set up to be moderately comfortable, and I was given a few servants.' Again, she shook her head. 'None stay long. Their tenure is dependent on their abilities as spies, I suspect.'

It was an appalling story of cruelty and deceit, Tam thought and wondered how she had endured and survived all these years. Another girl gently reared would never have done so, any other girl who was not Bothwell's daughter.

She said, 'I am also under the care and protection of Doctor Linmer, who is treated with respect by the Earl not only as a good physician, but a valuable alchemist supposedly working on experiments to turn gold from a stone.'

She laughed at that preposterous idea. 'And I have two formidable guardians who none would tackle willingly.' She indicated Zor and Mags, then sighed. ' I am now twenty and most girls are married earlier, but I have resisted all demands and attempts.' She paused and looked fondly again at Zor. 'Few would attempt to marry me by force, not with Zor here or risking the curses of Bauble Finn.'

She laughed. 'Dear Baubie, a kind woman who is treated by the Earl with care. She is perhaps a witch, but is very helpful with remedies and spells and as such greatly respected by his sons and any of their followers.'

She smiled and followed Tam's uneasy gaze to the creatures by her side. 'My uncle likes to believe they are domestic pets kindly provided for my comfort, but I see you have already noticed the significance of their presence as bodyguards. Zor was already here, a wolf-dog living in Baubie's cave, when I arrived.' Pausing, she stroked his head fondly. 'We took to each other immediately.'

Tam considered Zor anew. Certain that wolves in the wild did not survive many years suggested that as a crossbreed Zor must be a great age for large dogs. At a possible eighteen, was still strong and as exuberant as any puppy he had ever encountered.

'You have no idea how old he is?'

Marie shook her head. 'Nor can Dr Linmer say for certain. He just vaguely remembers that Zor was already here, fully grown, when he first came to the island.'

And Linmer was a time traveller who had got lost long ago he was a little confused about exactly when.

'Perhaps Baubie will know,' Marie said. 'Baubie brought me Mags.'

'Caw!' said the magpie, who seemed to be taking an acute interest in every word being said. Marie reached out and patted her head.

'Baubie found her with a broken wing, nursed her back to health and, although she will never be able to fly or catch her own food, she can manage very well indeed.'

'Caw!' said the magpie appreciatively, as Marie stroked her fondly and kissed her head. 'I do love my two pets. I am never lonely with them near.'

How pretty she was, Tam decided as she laughed again, just like a normal twenty-year-old. But pretty was the wrong word. Inadequate to describe this girl who had been shaped by ill fortune from her earliest days and had survived, with the inherited strength of her father and generations of the Border clans rather than her mother's weak and unlucky Stuart kings.

'I need not concern myself,' she said. 'Their presence keeps the curious at bay, and everyone at the Earl's court, as well as his own vast family of sons, have superstitions enough to keep away from the broch. Well known for their debaucheries, they venture only as far as Baubie's cave to plead for cures for syphilis and other distressing complaints. Even for the simple peasants, the honest citizens of Kirkwall, Baubie's cures are famous throughout Orkney.'

Tam was escorted by Ina and Zor to the room he would occupy. He found it comfortably furnished with a narrow bed, chair and table, along a corridor a short distance from that of Dr Linmer, in the only furnished part of the broch. His new surroundings were pleasant enough for a short stay in his temporary role as Master Edward Hepburn, uncle and tutor to Lady Marie. He considered how he might make the best of a bad job and reconcile mistaken time travel to Orkney with his original plan of Victorian Edinburgh.

Looking out of the narrow window past Baubie's cave towards the sea, he considered again his interview, this first meeting with the Queen Mary and Bothwell's ill-fated child.

He shook his head, seeing nothing but trouble ahead, already recognising the danger of his position as the new tutor most possibly being used to spy for the Earl, in his path to the ultimate goal: the throne of Scotland.

Meanwhile, Marie was also considering her first impressions of this new arrival. Even exercising her unused female charms as a royal princess, she had enough in good looks to have tried luring him into some plan to help her escape. Although a little old for her in the role of lover, his mysterious air and attractive appearance intrigued her. She sighed. She had had little opportunity for romance beyond the exploits of those characters recorded in the pages of fiction provided by the good doctor from his extensive library of the classics.

She replayed her short conversation with Tam Eildor and concluded that he was infinitely more fascinating than any of the knights found in books. His looks for one thing. He was certainly handsome as any portrait she had ever seen or remembered from the past, but his eyes mystified her. They reminded her of someone or something. She was falling asleep that night when Zor settled at her bedside and Mags ruffled sleepy feathers on a perch.

Marie sat up to blow out the candle, when Zor stirred and looked up at her. The eyes that met hers were also the eyes of Tam Eildor.

CHAPTER FIVE

A tap on Tam's door announced Linmer.

'The news of your arrival as milady's uncle and tutor has reached the Earl and he wishes to see you forthwith. He is not providing transport; a carriage might be considered an inducement for escape by a guilty man.' He smiled wryly. 'You go on foot or on the horse we have in the stables here.' Tam's startled glance told him what he had been expecting to hear. 'You don't ride?'

Tam shook his head. 'I've never been on horseback.'

'Well, now's the time to learn how to stay on,' Linmer said cheerily. 'Clover is gentle. Marie exercises her with a daily trot along the beach on fine days.'

Pausing to take a seat at the window, he continued, 'Before you leave to make your acquaintance of the Earl, it would be as well for you to know what things are like in Orkney and why you might get black looks. The way things are run here is appalling.

'Mary, Queen of Scots, was always generous to her father's illegitimate sons and often the daughters too. Marie's resemblance to her mother was unmistakeable. As soon as Earl Stewart set eyes on her, he recognised that the rumour of her as a surviving twin must indeed be correct, since it fitted place and time.'

Limner relayed the story of how the dukedom of Orkney had been left vacant during Bothwell's exile, in part already told to him by Lady Marie the previous evening. Linmer continued, 'King James created the Earldom of Orkney and from that point we were left to the tender mercies of Earl Robert. To describe in full the evils he has inflicted upon us is almost impossible.

'Skat or rent was always paid in kind and the old Norse weights and measures used to assess the right amount, but the Earl swiftly set about altering these to his own gain so that tenants were cheated and impoverished. People were imprisoned even executed without trial; dead men were tried for real or trumped,-up offences, their goods or estates confiscated, and all free intercourse of ships across the Pentland Firth was stopped, lest some voyager should carry the story of oppression to the authorities in the south, in Scotland.

'Free people are now forced to labour for the Earl without pay, as though they are serfs or slaves. The old udal laws and institutions have been twisted and altered to suit the Earl's selfish purposes. The udallers or landowners have been ruined, their lands confiscated and given out under feudal law to the Earl's many sons or hangers-on.'

Tam was remembering Linmer's words, as he prepared to travel to Kirkwall and meet the Earl, eyeing with some trepidation the horse that had been provided. Horses were few in his own time and as hobbies only, but here it was the only way to travel for most folk. Considering the roads, or lack of them, carriages would be in short supply and beyond the means of Orkney's impoverished citizens.

He patted her firmly and said, 'We are off now, Clover,' in what he hoped was an encouraging manner. They were watched by Linmer with some amusement, and something else.

'Take care!' Linmer shouted, but that seemed unnecessary. 'Looks as if he's been doing it every day of his life,' he muttered to no one in particular, watching Clover trot off down the road from the broch.

Tam discovered that he was quite comfortable in the saddle and prepared to enjoy yet another new experience in this strange world. He had forgotten that there would be no trees, at least none worthy of comment, or sheltering charm, like the sturdy oak, horse chestnut and elm he had associated with the ancient paintings of this lost planet before it was swallowed by disaster, an apocalypse brought about mostly by man's own negligence.

We always destroy the things we love, he thought, and in this case, it was centuries of turning a blind eye to the scientific discoveries of a rich environment that would turn upon man and destroy the air he breathed. Orkney was an island, to a certain extent it had escaped the destiny of Planet Earth's, leaving the only trees bold enough to inhabit these cold north-west isles, the timid sycamore and melancholy willow. Offering no airs of protection or benevolence, they hugged close to house walls in a manner suggesting despair and apprehension, their continual fight for survival clearly visible in twisted limbs.

The island lacked the splendour of those ancient Highland glens Tam had seen pictures of, but there was adequate compensation in wild beauty and infinite space, the great confluence of sky, sea and rolling landscape, undulating hills in a sea-bitten, wind-torn pastiche of greens, greys and peat browns interrupted here and there by a patchwork of scattered crofts, few out of sight or sound of the eternal sea.

Here the weather dictated fashion and turned its face against exterior ornamentation, which would soon succumb to wild winds and winter storms. For centuries past architects learnt the value of concentration on thick no-nonsense walls, deep-set doors and windows turned away from the sea, offering protection from merciless weather in a style set down by ancient brochs in that unrecorded slice of island history. Here and there he noticed the interruption of a stretch of emerald grass, the dangerous bogland Linmer had warned him to avoid.

Acutely aware that he was witnessing the mystic fulfilment of an ancient life long lost, Tam stopped and listened to that everlasting sound, night and day, storm and calm, the boom of wave on rock and shore. In one brief moment, in the susurrus of the sea's eternal song, he was hearing the whisper of creation, beyond time itself.

The sea was far below. And the seals were there. Following his progress with almost human intelligence, inquisitive, vigilant, with round, shiny bullet heads, sleek and grey, and shining eyes that looked strangely human.

Tam found himself remembering Linmer's parting words, like a kind of benediction, but his ruminations were rudely interrupted as he found himself flying through the air, the horse going one way and he the other. His yell 'Clover!' went unheeded, as the horse was already scurrying on to the safety of dry land.

Too late he noticed his legs were sinking, surrounded by the bright emerald of bogland he had been warned about and paying for that lack of attention to the directions of where he was going. In a strange place, having allowed the horse to take its head had a deadly cost. He had wandered into the marshland that separated the peninsula from the town of Kirkwall.

Although apparently unhurt, he attempted to struggle to his feet, only to discover that his legs were being sucked down by some determined and invisible source.

He stretched an arm free, but the panic button on his wrist was covered in thick mud. It refused to work, and with a groan of dismay, he remembered the rule. That he had to be on the beach where he had landed to be transported safely back to this own time.

His calls for help seemed futile. There was no one in sight.

CHAPTER SIX

In that deserted landscape, none but the birds heard Tam's cries for help. Their song interrupted for a few moments to make sure this danger did not threaten them, then it began again with renewed vigour.

As for Tam, despair seized him as he seemed to be sinking further inch by inch, his limbs slowly swallowed by encroaching mud.

Soon it would reach his waist.

Waving his arms about in a weary gesture, trying to keep them above the green horror devouring him, he stopped struggling for a moment.

There was the unmistakeable sound of approaching horses.

Somehow, his calls for help had been heard.

'Help me! Over here!' he yelled.

One of the riders had dismounted and a sheathed but

strong sword was being thrust towards him with the shout, 'Cling on and we'll get you out!'

There were other less cheering voices from the other riders, amidst laughter and catcalls. 'For God's sake, brother, just kill him, brother. Let the bog have him. Put him out of his misery. Aye, let's get on our way, we've delayed long enough.'

His rescuer was a young man in some sort of uniform, a short velvet cloak trimmed with ermine, echoed by the other riders, who were laughing and calling insults. There were five of them, and in sudden panic, Tam realised that he was unarmed and now surrounded by the Earl's notorious sons.

They moved closer, keeping their horses carefully away from the edge of the bogland.

'Is that him?' one demanded.

'Is that our escaped prisoner?' shouted another.

'Doesn't look much like a pirate.'

'Met him once. That creature is definitely not him.'

'Morham has a beard.'

A pause. Then, 'Kill him anyway,'

'Save time, push him back in the bog.'

'Nay. Father will want his head. Up on the castle wall. A warning—'

The argument continued and advice was ignored, until with a sudden heave, Tam's legs were free and he was staggering with the support of his rescuer to the safety of dry land that bordered the marsh. It was then he noticed that the young man was slightly lame, but that had not deterred him wrestling with the bog's deadly suction.

Tam's rescuer considered him carefully and shook his head.

'How did you do that?' he asked, amazed at the speed with which the apparently helpless man had moved. 'You are unhurt.'

'Thanks to you.' Tam looked round. 'But I seem to have lost Clover.'

'You have her to thank that we found you. A riderless horse in a panic always means someone in trouble.'

The man was good-looking. His yellow hair and nice manner didn't identify him as one of the wicked lads Tam had been warned about as he went on, 'Your horse was in a great hurry to get past us so I knew something was wrong. She got a shock too. I imagine she will be on her way back to her stable. That's the way with animals, they always seek safety.'

His smile was friendly and Tam said, 'Thank you again. You saved me from a very nasty situation,' he added.

'You wouldn't have drowned. It is no more than a few feet deep and you are tall.' His companions had vanished, after a few mocking curses, with no more interest once their advice to kill the trapped man had been ignored. No more than the entertainment of watching the dying struggles of a trapped animal at bay.

'You must forgive my brothers,' the young man said. 'They are idiots. We were sent out to search for this pirate who escaped. He was due to be hanged tomorrow.' He held out a hand regardless of the mud on Tam's own. 'I'm Owen – Owen Stewart,' he said, and Tam realised his lucky escape being reached first by one of the Earl's less ruthless sons. 'If you'd like to share my horse, I will take you to wherever you are going.'

Tam decided not to mention the Earl. 'I was going into Kirkwall, but I've changed my mind.'

Imagining that Tam had been shattered by his recent ordeal, Owen said, 'You would need to get rid of some of that mud,' he said tactfully. 'If you prefer, I'll take you back home. Where do you bide?'

'That's very good of you, sir. I stay in the broch, just across the horizon there.'

Owen's eyes brightened. 'The broch. Then you know Lady Marie,' he added in a tone of awe.

'Indeed, sir, I am her tutor.'

'The one my father is expecting from Scotland sometime?' Owen sounded excited by this news, and Tam decided caution was needed. From what he knew of the debaucheries of these sons of the Earl, he had already decided against taking Linmer's advice and introducing himself as Edward Hepburn.

'Her uncle, are you not?'

'Alas, no. I am Tam Eildor, a lawyer from Edinburgh, a survivor of the shipwreck. Master Hepburn and I were colleagues, but sadly he drowned.'

He was surprised at the young man's reaction. Owen looked relieved, even delighted, as he gave him a heave up onto the horse.

They began the short journey back in silence and so Tam was left to his own thoughts. Now there were fields where black and white cows grazed contentedly and sheep, long past endearing lambhood, hopefully

53

suckled mothers short on temper and long dry of milk.

All around them, the hedgerow bloomed with cow parsley and ragged robin, and other strange flowers, like lupine and pansies, the dark heath spotted brightly with bog cotton's fluffy tufts, pink sea drift and the shells of flag irises.

It was a scene that inspired him to poetry, a feeling he had never experienced before as above the sky was busy with a constant traffic of seabirds wheeling overhead that extended his awareness of the kaleidoscope of colour. Existing alongside muted shades of grey, blue and green, warm air brought the fragrance of small plants and wild herbs, and every blade of grass in every ditch as they rode by held an army of stealthy insects winged in rainbow hues and filling the air with vibrant music beyond human hearing.

Far into the endless blue overhead, skylarks heartened by another blast of sunshine added their flute notes of joy, while flocks of small birds, exhausted by rearing young, were returning home to happy celibacy.

At his side, Owen Stewart was experiencing quite a different but equally passionate emotion. Rescuing this man who shared his horse had been a streak of good luck, for at last he was to have the longed-for excuse to see Lady Marie Hepburn again. He had fallen in love with her at their first encounter on the beach when he had been sent down with a message from his father to Dr Linmer, who had somewhat unwillingly introduced them.

He had thought she was a servant and, without the least knowledge that she was the princess, he was soon in dismay, aware that she was to be married to his eldest brother, newly widowed Patrick, who despised him, as did his father and his other brothers. As the runt of the litter, he had been mocked since he could first remember by everyone in the Earl's court for his slight lameness.

As the horse trotted towards the broch, Linmer appeared and, fearing the worst, cautiously bowed to the Earl's son while Tam dismounted and explained what had happened. Linmer said that Clover had returned safely while at the same time observing with some disquiet that Owen Stewart was gazing round anxiously. Doubtless the boy was hoping to see Marie. He was relieved when she did not appear and, with no excuse to linger, Owen prepared to leave.

If only he could leave a message, if only . . .

Tam had some experience of the lovesick and had already interpreted his rescuer's nervous glances in the direction of the broch. Poor lad.

Owen leant down from his horse, Tam shook his hand and thanked him again. 'Glad I was to be of assistance, Master Eildor, and that you were not our escaped pirate,' was the response. He cast another pleading glance upwards to the broch, then one more towards the inscrutable Dr Linmer, hoping for that invitation to linger.

Owen gave a wistful smile. 'Perhaps we will meet again.'

With that he reined in and, looking down at the old man and the new tutor, he was on his way before he realised a quite extraordinary thing. As Tam saluted him, the mud from that immersion in the bogland had entirely disappeared, revealing well-polished thigh boots, leather breeches and an immaculate white shirt.

CHAPTER SEVEN

While all this was happening, a short distance away across the peninsula in Kirkwall Castle, Earl Robert was gnawing his lip, anxiously awaiting the arrival of Lady Marie's new tutor. He was not used to being kept waiting. He was looking forward to meeting Master Hepburn for secret reasons, and someone would suffer for this delay. Considering the princess's matrimonial future, he would have willingly married her himself regardless of the church rules of consanguinity. With the throne of Scotland as the potential goal, he rather fancied being King instead of Earl and regretted that one of his sons would have the privilege. If any of them was strong enough to deal with the responsibility, which he doubted, Patrick was best. He was recently widowed but had a demanding mistress, who called herself Countess and, although a trifle common, claimed descent from a noble Scottish family.

News of the wreck had already reached him and he realised that Edward Hepburn was most likely drowned. That was a nuisance as he had great hopes of learning of the fate of that Spanish gold sent by King Philip of Spain to pay for an invasion of England. This would be of particular interest to King James of Scotland.

At the moment of Tam's dramatic arrival at the broch and his rescue two days ago by Zor, a very troubled Earl had been sitting by a table in his castle surrounded by maps of the Bishop's Palace down the hill and next door to the equally ancient but well-maintained St Magnus Cathedral, its rose-red stones a little worn by time. Overlooking the scene below, he was considering his plan to replace the uncomfortable seat of bishops and his equally uncomfortable castle with a fine palace of his own.

The price would cost the islanders, scurrying in the streets like ants far below, dearly, though insects would have troubled his conscience and warranted consideration more. The consequence of this proposed building would doubtless bring about the loss of many labourers' lives, bereaved families and numerous men maimed, but his main concern was how and what further he could squeeze from his tenants; their rents, taxes and the miserable hovels of his already starving Orcadians would be required to pay for the magnificent palace as well as the ruinous expenses incurred by the recent unannounced visit by King James.

Far from being dismayed by this ruin of the national economy of Orkney the King had been impressed, since the

Earl's miserly streak was a condition that met his approval, as did anything concerning the magic word: gold.

Only gold was the magnet that had brought about this royal visit all the way from Edinburgh, very costly to the Earl's purse, but he was aware that His Majesty would go to any lengths, murder included, to obtain that still elusive Spanish treasure trove.

The Earl was soon to learn that the urgency of the royal visit was the information rumoured from spies in England that King Philip's gold was to have been delivered to a mysterious but safe destination in Scotland, but had disappeared on the voyage. Just a few miles south of Edinburgh, the stormbound vessel had sought refuge in a castle on the coast. Pursued by the English fleet it had made a hasty departure and abandoned its treasure in one of the castle's many secret caves. The intention was to outwit pursuers by heading north through the dreaded waters of the Firth across to Orkney. There they would anchor and, when the panic subsided, return to collect the gold from the owner of the castle, one Robert Logan of Restalrig.

The ship had never reappeared, and Earl Robert was pretty certain, aware as he was of all comings and goings relating to matters concerning Orkney, that it had never reached Kirkwall or Stromness.

King James was not convinced and regarded the Earl's reasoning with suspicion. Here was a man who shared the same devotion and dedication to the acquisition of gold as himself and, via his own highly efficient spy network, rumour had connected the treasure with a certain castle of ill repute and a Spanish ship wrecked there carrying Philip's invasion gold.

Time was of the essence, hence the informal royal visit, and the necessity of secrecy, costly as it was, ensured no expense was spared by either party. King James decided that as the Earl might be hiding something, the cunning answer would be to send him, or most likely one of six sons as well as his numerous bastard sons, in search of the gold, carefully watched over by a royal spy.

Under the careful scrutiny of his monarch, Earl Robert had unfolded an invaluable map, a copy of that charted by the Frenchman, Nicolas de Nicolay to the Firth of Clyde from the Firth of Forth. Through uncertain waters the King James toured his kingdom, seeking to quell unrest and pacify troublesome factions in the Western Isles. With intricate care and careful illustrations, the map presented in minute detail the nation's headlands, inlets and archipelagos. The map's precision made it an invaluable asset to travellers by sea and in 1547, it had reached French hands and was used by Henry II's forces navigating St Andrews to avenge the murder of Cardinal Beaton.

King James had studied the east coast of Scotland with its many castles and identified the most likely, one known as Fast Castle, perched on a high cliff a few miles from Edinburgh. It was almost inaccessible, the haunt of smugglers and Papist spies, with many secret caves in which to hide a Spanish treasure. Originally known as False or Faux Castle, it owed a sinister reputation to the light burning at night, high in its tower, to wreck ships on its rock-strewn shore. The only access to the castle was by a basket and a pulley or, on the landward side, over a large and tortuous scrubland from the drove road south from Edinburgh through East Lothian.

According to rumour and the few who knew its secrets, a less hazardous entrance existed by a cave leading up a flight of steep steps into the courtyard above.

It had to be the Spanish treasure which the castle concealed. The gold was of vital importance to King James, who knew more about his half-sister, Lady Marie Hepburn, virtually a prisoner on Orkney these twelve past years, than the Earl would have ever suspected. The royal spies also told of an old man, a supposed alchemist, in the Earl's employ, who guarded and educated Queen Mary's daughter.

The Earl hinted that this alchemist was a wizard, a role punishable by death in Scottish courts. This ruse concealed the real reason for his presence in the broch: to keep this valuable ward confined until the Earl could arrange her marriage and bring himself closer to the throne. Armed with this knowledge, King James was inspired to set forth a plan.

The king wanted him to produce gold.

'It is our wish' – for 'wish' he read 'command' – 'that your wizard goes to this Fast Castle and has a good search for Philip's treasure.'

The Earl had looked a little stunned as a thousand negative responses fought feebly through his brain. But even as he thought of a protest, the King's stern expression was his answer.

'Go to it with all possible haste,' were the parting words. 'We have great faith in your resources. It is well known that you can get blood from a stone.'

That might be a slight over-exaggeration, even for an alchemist, but the Earl did his best, an ambition hugely admired by his miserly King.

Watching the royal departure from the castle, those last words with their Latin tag translated roughly as: 'You can send one of your sons, their absence will not be missed.' The Earl groaned. He had more than enough problems with such a vast family depending upon him. As well as keeping them and their vast retinues in accustomed although somewhat old-fashioned elegance compared to the royal court at Edinburgh, they were constantly calling upon him for more money.

He sighed deeply. A trying time indeed and almost past his powers of imagination, which the King believed might bring forth gold from a stone or, in this case, a rumoured cave in an inaccessible island off the Scottish coast. He could already hear what their protest would be. He would send Owen; they would be glad to see their despised youngest brother burdened with this matter of state.

A noise in the courtyard below interrupted his thoughts. Shrieks and cries, and gusts of laughter, indicated the almost daily occurrence of the youngest son, Owen, being tormented by his brothers.

The Earl looked down on the scene. Patrick, the eldest, was certainly the best of his brood. He had inherited so much of his father, a mirror image in ruthless greed and craft, he needed to be taught no lessons in how he would eventually rule over Orkney. He was a lad to be proud of. His sons were the Earl's one weakness, and woe befall any citizen who would harm them by word, look or deed – or even rumour. The creature who did so, man, woman or even child, would pay by the loss of a hand, a tongue or with their lives. He was inordinately proud of such proof of his virility, but there was one exception; at the lowest and youngest of the six legitimate ones was Owen, the runt of the litter, who had a lame leg caused by an accident at his birth. This was regarded by the Earl as an unforgivable stroke of providence, a son who was not perfect in every detail.

Looking at Owen pained him deeply. He wished he had died in infancy and did nothing to avert the cruel behaviour and mockery of the elder brothers. For the folk of Kirkwall the whisper from those who had met him was that Owen was, in fact, the good apple in the bad barrel, and in his growing up had refused to follow the pattern of debauchery set by his father and brothers. To those citizens who could read and write, they kept careful watch over his developing years and knew that he loved books. From childhood he had escaped the confines of Kirkwall Castle and the merciless torments of his brothers, to spend much of his time with the boat builders, always keen to learn their craft.

Dismissed by his family and the adherents of the Earl's court as having inherited none of the warlike, scheming, quarrelling, gambling and other unworthy tendencies of his brothers on both sides of the blanket, Owen was used to being sneered at and scorned from his earliest days as a scholar only interested in reading and peaceful pursuits. If truth were told, and it was carefully avoided, his mother had been one of the powerful Percy family. Yet within days of Owen's birth, she had been sent back to Northumberland, as the Earl had found a new, more attractive conquest. Abandoned and forced to leave her baby, she fell ill and died on the ship in foul weather.

Owen heard the story whispered about the court and, once old enough to understand the reasons, he never ceased to blame his father, to condemn and hate him for murdering his mother.

But the Earl had already seen in the royal command to search for treasure a means to settle a score over a lady met at the wedding of Queen Mary to Lord Henry Darnley in Edinburgh. Now the King had given him the perfect, legitimate opportunity of settling it, deep-seated and kept fresh for twenty years, against one Robert Logan of Restalrig, owner of Fast Castle.

CHAPTER EIGHT

After the story of Tam's rescue had been told, Linmer watched Owen depart. 'The fact remains, the Earl is waiting to meet you,' he said sternly. 'Best not keep him waiting. Clover is in the stables. She came back covered in mud,' he added, surprised that Tam had not been similarly afflicted. 'We were very anxious about you.'

As Tam prepared to leave for a second time on Clover, who had eyed him with a reproachful snort as he saddled up, Tam thought of Linmer's words from his initial summons to the Earl's presence with considerable misgivings.

'You had better realise what you will be facing in Kirkwall. The inhabitants will not be out with flags of welcome and with good reason. An official document outlining their grievances was sent to the King years ago, a document that would have condemned the Earl and should have removed him from office. But to young King James, harassed by intrigues, those distant islands at the world's edge with their quarrelsome barons were but another wearisome task of little importance and the document was ignored. Truth to tell the miserly King admired his half-uncle's twisting the law's tail in order to gain the lion's share, but his consequent inaction over the years has cost many innocent Orcadians their lives.'

Linmer had sighed. 'It was a monstrous list of iniquities showing where the Earl had altered the old laws of the island guaranteed by the Scots parliament and added new enactments to suit his own purposes. Those who disapproved were banished, their property either confiscated or allowed to remain on condition they yielded up their heritages to him.

'Where these two methods of piracy failed,' he added bitterly, 'they were left to rot in prison without trial, despite the tears and entreaties of their families. The Earl further compelled lairds and lieges to entertain him and his household in a royal progress "to the number of six or seven score persons, with banquets and great cheer on their own expenses". As each of his children were rumoured to have a private army of retainers and followers, even a short visit led to their host's immediate penury and the inevitable transfer of his desirable property into the Earl's hands or whichever of his brood had cast a greedy eye upon it.'

Linmer continued, 'The diabolical list continued with misappropriation of common moors and pastures, and refusing to allow the burgesses of Kirkwall to trade except by the Earl's leave and licence. Even churches were not exempt, since the clergy were compelled to set their benefices to him. A more sinister form of subtle oppression was the increase of "bismer and pundlar", the ancient Orkney weights, to his own specification, which ruined landlord and small tenant alike. The price of meat was raised so that none could afford to buy it.'

As Tam remembered that list of grievances and the desperate straits of the islanders he saw the activities of the wreckers in a new light, now appearing as a necessity for survival.

'There was no escape by death, since dead men could be charged with old crimes, condemned in effigy and their goods confiscated. This left a margin for appropriating almost anything that took the Earl's fancy and showed a surprising depth of imagination. As for the live inhabitants, "none should leave Orkney and Zetland to make complaint against himself". And this was further reinforced by stopping all ferries so that none might leave without his licence.'

Without further disasters, Tam reached his destination. Although the weather looked kindly upon Tam, as he rode Clover up to the castle, the town appeared a clutch of sad-looking grey-stone squat hovels with flagstone roofs to protect them, further protection offered by being built in the shadow of the castle walls, and almost windowless from the treacherous elements.

A mere cluster of dwellings around the harbour formed by the Peerie Sea and a sandbar known as the Ayre hugged the shore to the edge of a main thoroughfare leading to the Bishop's Palace, which he rode past first, only slightly more ruinous in appearance than the Earl's castle on the hill. Only the ancient rose-red cathedral of St Magnus had managed to retain dignity and grandeur in these troubled times.

Riding down a long, cobblestoned street, Tankerness House was the sole mansion of any distinction. As for the castle, its approach was unassuming, its exterior sadly neglected over the years and appearing partly ruinous. This was echoed by the state of the interior and alleys where guards turned suspiciously towards Tam, making him feel more like a prisoner about to be convicted that a new arrival on the island.

If he had expected to be ushered into the presence chamber of a man about whose villainous reputation he had heard in some detail, then he was to be mistaken. Imagining that passing years, debaucheries of age and the tyranny equal to any of the Caesars of ancient Rome had turned the Earl of Orkney into a fairy-tale ogre, his appearance as Tam approached was not in the least extraordinary. The fine Stewart eyes, although never still, darting fiercely around the room, were recognisable, and the loose, sensual mouth proclaimed that Robert Stewart was also strong and virile in middle age.

Impressed by the splendour of the Earl's robes, the predominance of velvet and fur, silks and satins, all lavishly bejewelled, that marked his assembled family as members of an old-fashioned royal court, if Tam also expected the chamber to be grand, he was disappointed. The magnificent costumes served only to increase its shabby gloom.

There was a general air of lassitude, untidiness and indeed distinctly unpleasant smells that hinted at lack of washing. Male sweat prevailed and it came from the direction of a table at which the five young men, presumably brothers and the earl's sons, were somewhat noisily playing cards.

The whole room was heavy with the scent of wine, like a much-frequented tavern, and although the straw-strewn floor had covered in rugs, they too had suffered from the neglected attention of vomiting males and urinating dogs.

It was not a happy sight, and as all eyes were turned to Tam, who had at last been announced by a servant, the Earl swung round in his elaborate throne-like chair to regard his arrival from under heavy eyelids.

'So, you are the new man, Master Hepburn.' His eyes narrowed. 'We were led to believe you drowned in the late wreck from Edinburgh.'

'I was fortunate to survive. I managed to swim ashore,' Tam lied.

'Aye, is that so now?' The Earl gave this inconsequential escape due consideration and swung round to regard the table occupied by his sons, who had also found the newcomer an interesting proposition.

'Well, lads, what think you of our lady cousin's new tutor? Is he not comely for such a dour occupation?' His lips twisted, leaving no doubt what thoughts were going through his mind as coarse laughter erupted.

Tam regarded them coolly. He would not betray embarrassment to this wolf-like pack of youths, although that was clearly the Earl's intention.

'Speak up, Patrick. We await your opinion.' He laughed and pointed to a young man, clearly the eldest, doubtless his favourite and most like his father in looks.

Patrick left the table and sauntered over, to survey Tam from the purple velvet chair enthroned by his purple valeted father. The colour worn by all the family was sacred to them. On pain of fine or disfigurement no others were allowed to wear purple.

Tam kept his eyes on the Earl, deciding even at that distance that for Patrick to have earned such an unsavoury reputation, he must have begun his infamy in the cradle. He had nothing to denote wickedness in a face still beardless under butter-coloured hair, his appearance marred only by eyes so close-set they appeared to squint.

Leaning on the arm of the chair, Patrick regarded Tam, who on closer scrutiny now saw in a leap to the future hints of what lay ahead: how loose living, overindulgence and debauchery would turn him into a model of his father, another tyrant bred for Orkney, if he survived to middle age.

Eyeing Tam critically, the Earl spoke imperiously. 'Speak up, lad. He is keeping us all waiting.' There was a threatening note to his voice that received answering nods from the card table. 'We will make him sorry, will we not, if he wastes our time.'

This conversation was carried on contemptuously as if Tam was not indeed present, but although he was angry and discomfited, he would not let it show.

He did not attempt to break the silence that followed. 'Have you all lost your tongues?' the Earl demanded.

'I was just thinking, Father.'

'Then do not take too long about it, any of you. You are all reminding me of Owen, your rat-faced brother, who takes for ever to think about what he should eat next.

So, Owen was the missing number six. Tam felt he knew what lay ahead and despised and scorned such occasions for his father and brothers showing their wit, if such could be called, at a visitor's expense.

He was not one to stand there wringing his hands and looking embarrassed, wondering what to say next. He stood firm and, turning his back in Patrick's direction, asked coolly: 'What is it you require of me, sir?'

This was clearly not what the Earl expected; there was a strange, unexpected quality about this stranger, this Hepburn from the Borders. The man before him knew his own value and would not be diminished.

There was an air about him that Robert felt and saw clearly was missing in his own sons, although he looked not much older than them. He must be at least in his mid-thirties. None of the Stewart brothers had ever had such distinguishing characteristics; those dark, luminous eyes made him feel uncomfortable and he did not care to be made feel thus.

Angrily he snapped his fingers and the door opened to admit two burly courtiers. For a moment Tam's heart misgave him. Was he here to be arrested on some trumped-up charge and thrown into prison having decided to tell the truth regarding his identity? He'd told Owen Stewart as much as was needed: that his name was Tam Eildor and he was a lawyer from Edinburgh. The fewer lies the better, otherwise they tended to multiply exceedingly, one leading to yet another.

CHAPTER NINE

It was not to be so. Lies were not needed nor prison intended as Tam discovered with some relief merely the command to accompany the Earl on a walk in the gardens.

These peaceful surroundings were well chosen as a place for conversation away from the overcrowded atmosphere produced by his raucous sons' behaviour. It seemed that even their father had his limitations.

Tam was not long kept in suspense of the reason he had been withdrawn, , as the Earl paced through the herbs and roses leading a timid life fighting for existence in a multitude of weeds behind the garden walls. Head bent thoughtfully, arms behind his back, the Earl grunted occasionally as if at some unseen enemy or unpleasant thought, pausing occasionally to stare balefully at the castle windows. He need not have worried about being overlooked or overheard since they were dimmed with the dust of passing ages, while Tam took the opportunity to glance nervously at the two well-armed henchmen walking a few paces behind.

At last, the Earl stopped, his smile less effective at reassurance, just inches away and accompanied by a wave of bad breath.

Hands on hips, he regarded Tam sternly. 'Well, I'm waiting. You're safe enough here.'

Puzzled, Tam managed a polite bow. 'Waiting, sir?' he asked.

'Aye, man, waiting. Come now, spit it out.'

'I – I do not understand you, sir.'

In answer the Earl seized his arm, shook it impatiently, growling like a bad-tempered dog. 'Dinna pretend wi' me, you impudent nincompoop. What er – information have you for me?'

'Information, sir?'

The Earl shook his head wearily. 'I was led to understand that for a small – er – pension you would be willing to pass on certain useful information.' He paused to see the effect of this and shrugged. 'Just any wee bits of knowledge, any mortal thing that you regard might be of advantage to me.' Another pause, a frown. 'In my interests . . .' and the rest in a rush, 'And of course, concerning Lady Marie.'

Tam swore under his breath. So much for the deceased father's cousin, or whatever relation the tutor was to Bothwell. At that moment he was so indignant he would have willingly despatched Master Edward Hepburn himself, had not the Master Builder seen fit, in his infinite mercy, to rid the world by drowning a nasty sneaky villain.

'You wish me to spy for you, sir?' he said coldly.

The Earl nodded eagerly, shuffled his feet a little. 'Aye, that is so. To put the right word to it.' His grin revealed neglected teeth. 'As you have some acquaintance with the law, such persons come by information not readily available to ordinary folk, ye ken.'

Tam did not 'ken' in the least and, pleased by the Earl's discomfort, he bowed and said, 'You must excuse me, sir. I did not understand that I was engaged to spy' – he paused to emphasise the word 'spy' – 'on the late Lord Bothwell and Queen Mary's daughter.' Standing sharply to attention he managed to look down on the Earl by several inches and say stiffly, 'I am afraid your informants were mistaken. I am no spy.'

Drawing a deep breath, he continued, 'My name is Tam Eildor. I am a lawyer and I know little of Master Hepburn. We met in Leith and were fellow travellers on the ship that was wrecked a few days ago. Master Hepburn was drowned, unfortunately, but I was rescued by Dr Linmer and have been living at the broch until arrangements could be made for my return home.'

He paused. 'Having met you, sir, I had hopes that you might consider allowing me, in these sad circumstances, to replace Master Hepburn as Lady Marie's tutor.' And with a bow. 'I have adequate credentials.'

The Earl had listened and now regarded him with narrow eyes. This might be to his advantage. All was not lost. This one might be induced to spy.

Regarding his hesitancy, Tam said: 'If you do not consider that I am suitable, I wish to return to Edinburgh, but I cannot take ship to Leith without a signed pass.'

'Maybe, maybe in a wee while.' The Earl frowned, considering. He bit his lips a little, then revived and shook his head in what he hoped was a gesture of consolation. 'Aye, aye, the position is not without its rewards, Master Eildor.' Tam chose to ignore the mistaken name as he continued, 'Aye, a substantial pension, do not forget the pension. I am not asking you to wag your lugs for nothing.'

Tam hoped his stare indicated affront and insult. 'Sir, I would merely be wasting my time and yours. I must decline your gracious offer since I have never heard of anything suspicious in Lady Marie's behaviour. I can assure you that your ward' – he made the sound of the word with an accompanying twist of the mouth – 'is an innocent and virtuous young princess. Perhaps your enquiries would be more rewarding among the servants.'

'Not a chance, not a chance. Her few servants are entirely devoted. I have tried replacements through the years but they lasted mere days before she announced her dwindling needs required little help.' He laughed coarsely. 'As she is at pains to point out, there is little in the way of finery or jewels to employ servants, scant silver, or furniture or linen to tempt servants to thieve. If I put someone new into the kitchen, he or she would be immediately under suspicion and would learn nothing.'

He pointed a finger at Tam. 'You, Master Eildor, you were my last hope.'

Tam bowed. 'I shall be glad to serve Lady Marie for the shelter and the chance to earn a living here in Orkney,' Pausing, he shook his head sadly. 'I do not know how long it will last since my health is far from good.' Tapping his chest, he coughed experimentally and was pleased with the hollow sound. 'I wish only to spend my remaining time in peaceful meditation.'

'The more fool you,' said the Earl roughly, then he grinned. 'Aye, well, no spy is better than an unwilling one I suppose.'

'I assure you, sir, you are wasting your time since none can arrive or depart from the island without your knowledge—'

'Aye, aye. On another matter, keep your ears flapping for news of this Spanish gold.' The Earl paused, but Tam's blank expression suggested that this was news to him. With a disgruntled shrug, he continued, 'King Philip sent it to Scotland in an armed merchantman. Whatever kind of ship it was, both it and the treasure vanished into thin air.'

Tam was about to volunteer that had it come as far north, it most probably fell to the Orkney wreckers and that Spanish gold would now be at the bottom of the sea.

'A pity, indeed.' the Earl went on. 'If it had come up this way, and the witch wife, Baubie Finn, is a dab hand at conjuring up storms, it would have brought a ransom in gold that would have pleased His Majesty. Aye, a young king in years, but he has his head screwed on the right way—'

Patrick had approached, sauntering towards them, his curiosity aroused, since his father usually shared moments of importance with him. And truth to tell, Patrick was eager to know if his father had been similarly affected by Tam Eildor. There was something about this newcomer to the island that made him uncomfortable. It was not a quality that he had ever encountered before in the general run of life in Kirkwall.

Patrick knew that he was in the presence of a strong and powerful man. Was he a young man? He thought not. Although he looked no more than thirty-five, he had some indefinable air. Patrick gulped. Unless this was a quality that defined folk from the Border clans and Marie, apart from being royal, was certainly a very ordinary female, to the point of being boring, so he felt an urgent need to know more about this new tutor or spy, preferably before their marriage took place.

The Earl, aware of his son's presence, was saying, 'We will carry on this conversation anon, Master Eildor. You may leave us for the present and advise Doctor Linmer that we will be arriving at the broch to visit our ward on the morrow.' He paused to indicate Patrick. 'We have plans for her future that need to be discussed.'

Patrick found this amusing and smirked a little. His father darted him a sharp glance. 'We know what you have in mind. Your present whore, the noble countess, has always had an eye on the broch, a wee matter of compensation if not consolation.'

Patrick's smirk dwindled rapidly and, turning without another word, he returned to the table and rejoined his brothers.

'Inform Lady Marie to expect us to arrive, Master Eildor. Now you may go.'

Heading back to the broch, Tam was getting to know Clover and found riding easier than he had expected, adapting to the rhythm of a steady trot. In sunshine, the lilac-coloured sky heralded the approach of night.

Tam's thoughts were of tomorrows in this land, whose waiting was measured not in passing centuries but in the darker millennia beyond the ken of this new race that had evolved since Planet Earth collapsed. Orkney had survived, this island at the world's edge, feared as the home of wreckers, seal people, trolls and mermaids, but the earth's survivors had taken refuge on Mars, known as Planet B.

Looking round, Tam saw that man had been bold enough, here and there, and turning a blind eye on the vagaries of an unreliable climate had planted houses, perched uneasily as summer flies on hillsides and a boulder-strewn terrain stretching to the horizons.

As the broch beckoned on the peninsula and riding Clover had become an enjoyable experience, he suddenly realised the danger he was in. He hadn't given it much thought until this interview had revealed its true extent. Although he had told the truth and was no longer an impostor accepting the role of a dead man, a spy in the Earl's pay, the whole situation of his life in the broch was fast becoming equally hazardous.

As a sensible man, he should seize this opportunity of going back to the beach where he had landed and by touching the panic button on his wrist, return to his own time.

The broch came into view. Why not return this instant? He had landed here by no fault of his own in the wrong time, not only wrong but fantastic, like finding himself an unwilling captive in one of the Grimms' fairy tales. The other characters were perfect and suitably sinister. He should have been warned by Dr Erasmus Linmer, an impulsive but careless time lord now doomed to a lifetime – Tam shuddered to think how long might that be – here in Orkney.

He gave that a bit of thought, since it wasn't difficult to forget the way back as time travel had its rules and all memory of the year 2300 faded after the first hour. The traveller then lived by the rules of the time period he had chosen, allowed to carry nothing but the clothes on his back, no weapons or protection except what was then available and, the strongest rule of all, unable to change the course of recorded history by killing off a bad ruler or a dictator.

He thought again of his companions. No help there, except for the wolf-dog Zor, who had saved his life. A weird creature who read a man's thoughts and listened to conversations very attentively as if he understood every word. More than a little sinister as well was the predatory magpie, Mags, devoted to her mistress. Tam shuddered. He would hate to be on the wrong side of those sharp eyes and even sharper beak.

Another weird creature was the woman Baubie Finn. She undoubtedly had power and magic, but Tam decided apart from her excellent soup he was going to steer well clear of her spells. Halcro, that fisherman husband, seemed quite normal, though how on earth had he got landed with her Tam would never understand. Halcro could have told him that her magic included being a lovely young woman to some when she felt like it.

They were the odd characters. The other most important role, standard fare in any fairy tale, was the captive princess in her castle, in this case the broch.

He sighed. The obvious answer for him would be to fall in love with the princess and by some magic, release her from the enchanter's spell. He hadn't been provided with any magic, and in the role of the enchanter, a real-life evil villain: her uncle the powerful Earl of Orkney.

Another role was needed for the hero who came to her rescue.

Well, it isn't me, Tam decided. I am not the stuff heroes are made of. I don't care for endangering my life with deeds threatening life and limb. I am a scholar, not a fearless man of action. I'm, a bit of a coward, anything for an easy scholastic life, although I wouldn't admit that to anyone but my bathroom mirror.

Then suddenly he took heart. There was a real prince lurking about. Who but Owen Stewart, the Earl's youngest son, despised as a spineless slob by his brothers and his father for not participating in their evil ways. Yes, here was a young man with the makings of a fairy-tale hero, even to the point of being slightly lame.

And from what he had observed at their first meeting, a splendid honest young fellow in love with this real princess and eager to rescue her from her long imprisonment in the broch by the Stewarts and their intention to marry her off to Patrick, to whom Tam had taken an instant dislike.

At the broch, Zor appeared to greet him. Dismounting he patted Clover and, receiving an affectionate nuzzle in return, Tam wondered if Owen and Marie and their perilous future was the reason he had decided not to vanish this very moment as his feet conveniently touched the sand.

Linmer came out to meet him. 'Glad to see you in one piece, lad. What happened with the Earl?' Following him inside and outlining their meeting, Tam said, 'Master Hepburn was chosen as a spy.' Linmer looked gloomy when Tam added, 'Other bad news. The Earl is arriving with Patrick tomorrow. I suspect that has to do with arranging the marriage to Lady Marie.'

Linmer looked even gloomier. 'This is dreadful. We cannot possibly accommodate his entire court. We haven't the means or provisions.'

'I think he is well aware of that, and it won't be a state visit with his entire entourage of sons and their followers.'

Linmer nodded. 'This place could never accommodate them. He doesn't like the broch, knows well enough that it is highly uncomfortable, except for Lady Marie's rooms. I expect you are right, it will only be a short visit, enough to organise the marriage arrangements. Presumably they intend to take her back to Kirkwall with them.' He shook his head. 'Not a happy prospect. The castle is all a bit of a mess, I gather. At present he is concentrating on rebuilding the Bishop's Palace.'

He shrugged. 'Well, we must just wait and see what lies ahead.'

Tam wasn't consoled and, when the next day's event unfolded, he wished heartily that he had obeyed his instincts and pressed the panic button when he had the chance. He could have been safely back in his own time.

But he was too late.

From the shadows, a tall young man was emerging.

CHAPTER TEN

The stranger came forward and bowed, as Linmer said grimly, 'We have a visitor. This is Captain Morham.'

The man smiled as Tam said, 'I met the Earl's sons out searching for you.' Morham cast a bewildered glance at Linmer, indicating the need for an explanation.

Here was trouble indeed. Surely, they realised the danger of having a wanted man at the broch? Things were bad enough without sheltering a pirate sentenced to death. Morham certainly looked like a pirate: tall, with a singularly rakish look, a head of thick russet hair and brown eyes that touched a familiar chord.

Morham shook his head, ending the confused silence. 'I am no pirate,' he confirmed. 'I'm just from a merchantman whose vessel is anchored in these parts. Had no permit to enter Orkney waters, so I was thrown into prison. That is the Earl's way of dealing with such matters. However, I escaped thanks to Owen Stewart. He told me he had friends at the broch who would give me sanctuary, so here I am,' he ended with a cheerful smile.

'You are welcome, sir,' said Linmer solemnly. 'Owen is a good friend to us and has our welfare at heart.'

'I am glad to hear that as I gather he also has his reasons for needing a ship. Perhaps these are known to you?'

This question was directed at Linmer, who clearly didn't and shook his head.

As Morham talked he continued to regard Tam. When he had finished talking to Linmer, he frowned and said, 'I am William Hepburn from Morham. Master Eildor and I have met before.'

Tam shook his head. 'That is not possible, sir.' But he was now aware of that likeness. The man before him, William Hepburn, was obviously the son of Lord Bothwell, who had inherited his father's likeness, but his tall elegance and classical features were undoubtedly those of his Norwegian mother.

William smiled at Tam's puzzled expression and said, 'It was at Morham we met and you would not recognise me now. It was a long time ago and I have changed a lot.' He laughed. 'I was but four years old living with my grandmother and you came on a visit with the Queen. We had few visitors. I was very impressed and remember it clearly,' he added firmly.

Tam shook his head, but there was a trickle of memory, of strong emotion, pushing through. Had he been in love that day – with Marie Seton?

William continued, 'It was you, I am certain, Tam Eildor. Twenty-five years ago, but you are unchanged, even the clothes you are wearing. It is incredible.'

Tam insisted, 'You must be mistaken, sir.'

William said determinedly. 'No, no. I have an excellent memory. This is not only incredible, it is impossible.' He paused, clearly searching for a reason as he regarded the expressionless faces of the old man and this eternally young one. His immediate thought was witchcraft and yet there was nothing sinister about either of them.

Stroking his chin, he had the obvious explanation. 'Do you have a son, perhaps, sir?'

Tam straightened his shoulders with dignity and said, 'I am unmarried, sir.'

William grinned. 'That was not my question. Your reply was evasive. Children can be got, and frequently are, outside wedlock. Marriage is not a necessary prerequisite.'

Linmer had been observing the two men silently, now interrupted, 'Tell me again, Captain, about your escape. It is vital we know as the Earl is coming tomorrow.'

Meanwhile, for Tam, there was only astonishment and confusion. Here he was face to face with a man who, as a child, remembered him from an earlier time-travel episode. This was rare, but trouble indeed. His need for that panic button would never be greater.

He looked helplessly at Linmer, whose gentle nod as he patted Zor's head said that he would not tell William anything. Zor, as usual, looked almost human as he regarded the newcomer thoughtfully.

Tam had to be certain this was no mistake, the man before him was the son of Lord Bothwell. There was the hint of the ruthless strength of the Border revivers in Captain Morham. He could well imagine that the man before him was a pirate, but he was curious to know what had led him to such a reckless career, details that would doubtless emerge in due course.

'What brought you to Orkney, sir?' Linmer was asking.

He received a mocking glance. 'It so happens that we do a little trading.' He shrugged expressively. 'Not all of it legal, there's the trouble. We do not advertise the fact that the *Falcon* is a pirate ship and we fit in some smuggling as well as boarding tactics. That isn't easy with a small crew, even well-armed it has to be done by trailing and observation over many sea miles.'

Realising Linmer's look of disapproval, he grinned. 'We are at pains to rob the rich to give to the poor – the latter being ourselves of course, in the best traditions of folklore tradition. There are advantages in not bearing a black flag. However, we did fall foul of the Earl's watchdogs. All except my boson and I managed to escape.' He sighed. 'As you will have heard the news was widespread about a dangerous pirate and how any who give him shelter would suffer the same fate intended for him.'

In the pause that followed Tam interposed, 'How did you manage to escape?'

To which Linmer added, 'And to make your way here?'

William smiled. 'It was quite remarkable. When I saw my rescuer was one of the Earl's sons who issued a command that I be released, I thought my end had come. But Owen Stewart had his own reasons for sending me to the broch for sanctuary. Owen Stewart', he repeated, 'who I soon gathered has no love for the rest of his family. In prison I had already heard rumours of the Earl's misdealings and also of his royal ward who he plans to marry off to the eldest of his brood, his son Patrick.'

He smiled. 'This was a very interesting piece of information and the perfect opportunity to meet my half-sister' – he paused dramatically – 'Lady Marie Hepburn. I did not even know of her existence. I believed the story that, along with the tragedy that had overtaken the Queen and my father, the twins of their brief marriage had been born prematurely and died when she was imprisoned in Lochleven Castle. Then I heard the whisper by way of her loyal and devoted servants that a girl had survived. After the Queen left, they had kept this tiny morsel of humanity alive. I knew nothing further except what Owen Stewart told me, that she had left the various foster parents of her early years and, when the ship she was hoping would reach Lord Bothwell was captured en route, the Earl made her his ward. Though I gather he has kept her in custody here in the broch, not in his castle.'

And that was just the beginning rather than the end of her misfortunes, Tam thought grimly, regarding the machinations of Earl Robert for his own wily ends.

Tam interrupted with what was now a pressing problem. A visit from the Earl to arrange the immediate marriage of his eldest son Patrick to Lady Marie.

'Is this her wish?' William asked, remembering Owen's report.

'No. She has always resisted it,' Linmer said.

'She must have been exceptionally strong as a child to survive that hazardous voyage believing she would find her father waiting to welcome her, when in fact he was already dead, betrayed by all those he had believed in. This is monstrous.' He turned to Tam. 'This Patrick Stewart. What manner of man is he?'

Tam said, 'I am a newcomer here, sir. Dr Linmer can tell you more of his rumoured iniquities and those of the Earl's rule than I can. But let us say that Patrick is newly widowed to an unhappy wife who died in a loveless match and he already has one current mistress who has been with him for several years.'

Linmer interrupted William's shocked exclamation, 'We cannot delay. We must prepare for their arrival.' He paused and looked at William. 'But what are we to do with you, Captain Morham, before they arrive?'

William shrugged. 'An escaped prisoner with a price on my head. I fear my presence has added to your existing problems.'

'It has indeed,' Linmer said, pointing to Tam. 'Master Eildor here arrived without a permit from the ship that was wrecked, and in his own interests we suggested he should be one Edward Hepburn, uncle to Lady Marie who sadly drowned.'

Tam put in, 'The plan that I declined as having too many problems was that I should take on his identity as her tutor.'

'The shroud of a supposed deceased man,' William commented grimly. 'Always somewhat complicated, I can see that. I gather from what I have heard that my uncle is somewhat irascible and prone to violence.'

'That is so,' said Linmer grimly. 'But now you must meet Lady Marie—'

'My little sister,' William interrupted eagerly while Linmer wondered what her reaction would be to this arrival of her half-brother instead of the vaguely remembered Hepburn uncle lost in the shipwreck.

Linmer was a very worried man. How were he and Tam to conceal the presence of a wanted man in the broch from the Earl?

'First of all, sir, we will have Baubie Finn remove that beard, see if you look less like a pirate without it.'

'Who is this Baubie Finn?' William asked doubtfully.

'She's our local witch,' was the cheerful response.

William stroked his beard. He didn't believe in witches nor did he particularly care for beards and would prefer to be clean-shaven, but a beard was simpler for the pirate image and easier too.

If Baubie's strange appearance was a shock to him, he managed to conceal it very well, kissed her hand, no less charming than being introduced to a titled lady.

As for Baubie, who kept a careful eye on any newcomers, she had been delighted at the sight of a second handsome young man. Warm water and an evil-looking sharp knife were produced and, at his slightly alarmed look, she smiled. 'I have been doing this for my husband, Halcro, for more years than I can remember, so you need not worry, young sir, I am an expert.' She clearly was, taking great pains and enjoyment in the task.

As well as surprised, Marie was excited to meet William Hepburn, a very handsome young man, just a little older than herself, who was not only her half-brother but a notorious pirate known as Captain Morham. She was just a little disappointed that he did not look in the least like a dangerous outlaw, whose beard Baubie Finn had skilfully removed.

William took her hands with a gentle smile. 'My existence was merely to persuade Lord Bothwell to make their betrothal a legally binding marriage, so my mother followed him across Europe, determined to be recognised as she believed was her right in the courts of Europe,' he told Marie. 'My father was in continual flight from her, wishing only to serve Queen Mary, always a little in love with her. His reckless passion may have brought about the murder of her husband, Lord Darnley, and the eventual tragedy waiting for them both.'

He sighed. 'I had a happy childhood at Morham with my granddam, who truly loved and cared for me until she died in '72. Her family who inherited had children of their own. At fifteen I was in the way and they had never liked me nor my parents,' he added bitterly.

He and Marie had much to talk about and he was sad to discover that they had more in common than most siblings. Lady Marie was even more of an orphan than himself.

'My mother the Queen was so ill in captivity at

Lochleven, they believed she was dying, so it is doubtful if she ever knew that one twin had survived.'

Marie regarded William tearfully. 'Her heart was broken. Her forced abdication from the throne of Scotland, rejected by the country that had once adored her at Carberry Hill, torn apart from my father, never to meet again. Her distress was unimaginable and she had more than enough problems trying to escape imprisonment.

'I was kept alive by the determination and constant attention of the Queen's favourite and most devoted Marie Seton. When I was old enough to understand what happened next, I was told the dramatic story of my mother's failed plan to escape from Lochleven, how Seton took me for safety to her own home at Seton Palace before rejoining her beloved mistress.'

Marie smiled. 'And there I thrived and for those very early years I was passed down briefly from one Bothwell relative to another, living in a succession of castles and manor houses for bewilderingly brief periods.'

She stopped remembering again, the things she would never forget, a set of rooms that felt like home, enjoying the gardens and the company of other children, forming friendships with them, playing with their games and toys. Then suddenly it was over. She shuddered at the memories of being woken in darkness, hastily dressed by candlelight and without any explanation moved tearfully on.

'I missed their kittens and puppies most of all.'

William noticed that Zor was an eager listener to their conversation. He sat at Marie's side throughout and, sitting down, was even taller than she was, looking from one to the other as if he was already a participant eagerly waiting to be included, asked some question or other for verification.

Marie stroked him gently and he appeared to smile.

A weird creature, this massive animal, who seemed more like a human under enchantment. William shivered, especially as the bird called Mags had settled on Marie's chair and was regarding him with an air that might in a person be called intent and suspicious, occasionally pausing to sharpen her beak on the chair's wooden arm and ruffle her feathers like an indignant dowager, particularly when Marie had looked tearful at William's account of his childhood.

Their shared reminiscences had drawn them ever closer and, with so much still unsaid, they had no desire or will to part. Ina brought them refreshments, bread and cheese and ale, but although they ate politely it was a matter of indifference exactly what they ate. As dusk gathered around the broch and Ina lit the wall sconces, William suddenly realised the hours that had passed and took Marie's hands.

'My dear sister – may I call you that? – I am not here to stay, but I want to help you.' He paused, then said delicately, 'Dr Linmer tells me that you are about to be married.' As she shuddered, he asked, 'Do you wish to marry Patrick Stewart?'

She gave a startled exclamation as she pulled her

hands free and clutched them together.

'No, never. Never!'

'Then you shall not. You have my word, sister,' he said firmly.

'What can you do?' she wailed, having almost added 'a wanted pirate', as he straightened his shoulders and replied.

'I shall think of a way and I know I can rely on Dr Linmer and Master Eildor – and even the witch Baubie Finn – to help me,' he added, taking hold of her hands again in a firm grasp. 'With their help – and my ship – you shall escape from this dreadful place – this prison, as it has been for the past twelve years. Never fear, we will succeed,' he said calmly and confidently, although his ship the *Falcon* was at present inaccessible under the Earl's close guard.

She smiled, her expression one of hope for the first time. 'I know of someone else who will help.' Pausing, her gentle sigh confirmed his suspicions that the Earl's son who had released him from prison was enamoured of her and that the feeling was mutual as she declared: 'Owen Stewart, Patrick's youngest brother.'

William shook his head. 'That dreaded family.' Frowning, he demanded, 'You are quite sure that you can trust him?'

'I can. He loves me,' was the firm response. 'And he despises his brothers, who have made his life a misery. As for his father, he hates him. He blames Uncle Robert for his mother's death. She was one of the Percys of Northumberland and died when Owen was a few days old.'

'Another orphan.' William shivered. 'Like us. Sad orphans.'

He kissed her hands and held them close. 'What a fearful family we have. It's dreadful to be related to such folk.' He sighed. 'My granddam was all the world to me, the only family I ever knew. But when she died, the Sinclairs decided I should go. They weren't prepared to support me and considered I was old enough to make my own way in the world, my world that had been no further than the gates of Morham Castle. The most they would do, and expected me to be grateful, was to apprentice me to an Edinburgh lawyer and hope never to see me again.' He shrugged wearily. 'I often wonder if ordinary people are like that, so indifferent to those who depend on them.'

'I doubt that,' said Marie. 'I am told by Ina that most common folk are close bound, love one another and would sacrifice anything, even their lives, for their children.'

She paused for a moment to let William grapple with this novel idea and then went on. 'From Ina and servants who know about such things, there was one terrible case – another of uncle's cruelties – where one of his sons had raped their little girl, aged twelve. The mother complained to the Earl and asked for justice, but the son said it was a lie. Of course, he was believed and the child would go to prison and likely die or be burned as a witch for lying. Her mother immediately said no, she would take her place.'

'What happened?'

Marie shrugged. 'I don't know the end of it, but she may still be in prison.'

'A terrible story,' William said.

'But one of many, alas,' she replied. 'There is no end to the cruelty and wicked way the Earl rules over us. None can go against the laws he has made without risking not only their lives but their children being disinherited.' She paused to regard him reproachfully. 'When did you turn pirate, William?'

His reply was to wait as footsteps on the stairs announced the arrival of Linmer and Tam.

CHAPTER ELEVEN

Neither Linmer nor Tam had any ideas for how they were to sort out the problem of concealing the presence of escaped prisoner Captain Morham during the Earl's imminent visit.

Marie panicked, but after a short discussion it was decided that William should stay in the broch, as this would be the safest place, since neither the Earl, Patrick nor any of their entourage were likely to climb the spiral stairway to Marie's room. Or beyond, for William's concealment were the dark corners and embrasures of the original building, including one almost inaccessible gallery at the top of a narrow turret stairway.

This was Linmer's domain. In addition to his room more conveniently situated at the entrance to the broch, the gallery was his special place as an alchemist and astrologer. A window on the stars, it had accumulated over his years at the broch a wealth of books and papers, globes terrestrial and celestial, a drawing board, compasses, instruments, and a calculator.

Tam took William alias Captain Morham aside for a moment. The pirate seemed a likeable young man, but he remembered how the Hepburns were not to be regarded as entirely trustworthy. They went with the winds of change in their alliances and his thoughts lingered on the late Edward Hepburn, who as Marie's intended tutor was also a spy for the Earl.

Tam looked again at William. Piracy apart, the role of spy did not fit in with his identity as Marie's half-brother, but then one never knew. In his experience of time travel as well as the vast literature of past ages, many an honest, trustworthy face had concealed a devil.

He decided, as there was little time to waste, he must tell William of his conversation with the Earl in the castle gardens.

'I was there in the guise of a tutor for Lady Marie.' He paused. 'He believed that this man Edward Hepburn would be a willing spy. For a pension,' he added grimly.

'Edward Hepburn.' William frowned. 'I have never heard of him. Some distant Bothwell relation, I suppose. But the idea of spying on an innocent young girl and receiving payment for such despicable behaviour is appalling.'

Tam said, 'Dr Linmer's idea was that I should pretend to be Edward Hepburn, who must have drowned in the wreck, but I was against that. Just as well I was since Marie remembered her Uncle Edward as middle-aged, stout and bald. So I told him what Dr Linmer and I had finally agreed: I had met Edward on the ship, but I was Tam Eildor, a lawyer from Edinburgh who had been rescued by the doctor.'

Tam also added the rest of that conversation, that he was willing to tutor and if that did not please the Earl, all he needed was a pass to leave Orkney and return to Edinburgh.

'He gave that due consideration and expected me to keep him informed of any matters regarding Lady Marie and her background. In other words, a pension, for spying.'

William shook his head. 'Dreadful! I knew what Earl Robert was like, vague rumours of his tyranny had reached as far as Scotland that all was not well in Orkney. However, until I landed here, I imagined most of it was probably exaggerated.'

He paused and thought for a moment. 'When I was taken before him to be sentenced to death as a pirate, he asked me some peculiar questions, such as did I know aught of castles on the Northumberland coast where it would be possible for a ship to land a cargo.'

A cargo. And Tam had little doubt regarding the nature of the cargo that so interested the Earl. It was what Linmer had told him about: the mythical Spanish gold sent by King Philip of Spain to finance the invasion of England.

William continued, 'I was very apprehensive about what lay ahead, especially after all the questioning. I was then taken back to my prison. The fate of pirates is death by hanging. After my escape with young Owen's help, when I arrived here, Dr Linmer was particularly interested. The Earl had informed him that he was to be presented to King James, the idea being that as an alchemist, he could produce gold from a stone.'

He frowned. 'The King is just a year older than Marie, but from what you tell me and what I have heard rumoured, he is already obsessed with greed and power.'

In the silence that followed, the same thought occurred to both men. What sort of a reign lay ahead for the people of Scotland, a king who might turn out to be just another but even more powerful tyrant than Earl Robert of Orkney?

Tam asked, 'What brought you to here? Where were you heading before your ship was taken?'

William sighed. 'We do some, er, trading round the north coast of Scotland, even intending as far as Zetland if the weather between the isles, always uncertain, permits We were short-handed, some odd sickness had overtaken the crew and we put them ashore near Nairn hoping they would make their way somewhere they could receive medical help.'

He spoke with a certain hesitancy and seemed reluctant to discuss this trading business, which Tam read as privateering. 'We don't carry a physician,' he explained, which all sounded a bit vague to someone who didn't understand anything about seamanship or the eugenics of privateering.

They were alone now, sitting on a boulder in the shade of the broch. Linmer had scuttled way and Tam asked William what had also been intriguing Marie.

'Why did you turn to piracy?'

William smiled, rubbing his now clean-shaven chin as if he missed the beard. 'It's a long story,' and as he repeated what he had told Marie of his childhood.

He shook his head. 'One of the men I met after leaving home had a kindly nature and a trading vessel in Leith. He said they were always looking for crew and took me on as a cabin boy.' He smiled wryly. 'What I hadn't been told and was to find out was that the ship, once out of Scottish waters, hoisted the pirate flag and became a privateer.'

Watching the seagulls wheeling overhead he added, 'It wasn't an easy life, but I did what was required of me. I was a good sailor, worked hard, obeyed orders and made friends among the crew – graduating from running up sail masts and all the while learning seamanship and navigation, how to use a sextant. Hard work had been good for me physically and soon I was strong enough to help steer the ship in awful weather – and there was plenty of that.'

He paused, narrowing his eyes as he looked out over to the calm sea. 'The Captain liked me, knew he could trust me. He had lowly beginnings from being a cabin boy himself and he envied my education, barely able to read and write while I had a succession of tutors at Morham. We became friends—' he stopped and frowned. 'A couple of years later, he took ill. One of our raids had gone wrong and he was wounded in the regions of his stomach. Before he died, he left instructions and signed documents that, as he had no family, the ship was to be mine.'

He stopped and Tam asked, 'What about these raids on other ships? Did you continue them?'

William shrugged almost apologetically. 'It was the only seagoing I knew, the only way to survive.' And, turning to face him, Tam saw for the first time how the years had shaped this young man, that of his father Lord Bothwell taking precedence in his character and obliterating his inheritance from the Scandinavian nobility. His Borderer father would have been proud indeed to have a privateer as his son.

'One of my first voyages as captain was in rough seas, and we were blown on to the rocks of a castle down the coast near Edinburgh. I thought our end had come, as this particular castle is marked on the maps as Faux Castle and is to be avoided as it lives up to its name as a place of wreckers. But we had only minor damage and were made much at home.' He smiled. 'And there was my cousin, Francis Stewart, who had stayed with my granddam. Of a similar age to myself, we became firm friends as children. As for the owner of the castle, Robert Logan of Restalrig has a rather unseemly reputation.'

With a sigh, he added quietly, 'We are related. The present mistress of the castle is my Aunt Janet.'

He shook his head sadly. 'What a family we are! When last I heard, Francis had taken refuge with them. As the fifth Earl of Bothwell, he is an even more wanted man than Captain Morham.' He raised his hands in mock horror. 'He has been in and out of captivity in Edinburgh though the years, accused of conspiracy to kill the King.'

He laughed. 'He's safe enough in Logan's castle though, the boast being that it could, with twelve men inside its walls, withstand the siege of a whole army. I could see the truth of that when our ship approached it – on a pinnacle of fierce rocks with no safe place to land.'

His laughter had faded, his smile turned into a frown. 'For me, this is my last journey. I made a solemn promise to a lady in the Mearns. We met several years ago and we are betrothed.' The frown became a contented smile. 'She's an heiress, has recently inherited a fine estate in Aberdeenshire, but has always refused to marry me unless I quit the seas. Now there is an added reason, she needs a strong man to help her run the castle and the estate.'

He sighed. 'And I am happy to do as she wishes. Ten years at sea have been more than enough for me.' He was silent for a moment, frowning and thoughtful, and Tam had an insight into his mind, the accumulation of all those dire unlawful acts of a privateer, which as William Hepburn he would prefer to forget.

'So this was to be my last voyage and I had been to Zetland.' He refrained from saying why, but it was clear to Tam that the Scandinavian merchant vessels had been the target.

'We were blown in a fierce storm not towards the north coast of Scotland as we had expected and hoped, but on to Orkney. We knew they were wreckers but decided to take a chance on taking shelter when we were taken by the Earl's forces, stripped of our cargo and valuables and the *Falcon* seized. So here I am no longer with a ship.'

He gave a sad smile as he added, 'At least my loving Susannah will be pleased, as long as I can persuade the Earl to let me leave. What will become of my ship, I have no idea.'

Pausing, he looked intently at Tam and said, 'I have told you my story, now what is yours?'

Tam shook his head and William continued, 'Come now, I know it is impossible for anyone to believe or accept, but I am certain that you are the same man I met on the Queen's visit to my granddam at Morham when I was four years old. And yet, here you are completely unchanged, even wearing the same clothes I remember, almost a quarter-century later.' He looked at Tam, waiting. 'I am sure you must agree, there has to be some explanation.'

Again, Tam felt the uncertain quiver of memory, a memory that hurt. He had been in love that day with Marie Seton, one of the four Maries who had been with the Queen since her childhood. He couldn't recall exact details, for they belonged to his time-travel experiment, lost like a half-remembered dream as soon as he returned to his own time. But in this instance the emotion had been strong, the pain a tremor, the flutter of a bird passing overhead.

'Come now, Tam Eildor,' William repeated. 'We both know it was you.' He shook his head. 'Are you a wizard, for such things are impossible for normal beings?'

Tam was silent, biting his lip.

William put a hand on his arm. 'Rest assured, I mean

you no harm. I am sure you are a good man and whatever you tell me will remain a confidence between us.' He looking round. 'There are some odd things at this broch: Dr Linmer and Baubie Finn and a wolf-dog that would talk if he could speak.'

There was no answer. Tam was intent on watching the seabirds flying overhead and William continued, 'There is something very weird about this broch, but not devilish about you. You don't seem to – belong.' Pausing again, he shook his head. 'And I have found myself among strange beings on what seafaring men once shuddered away from – these isles at the edge of the world. You and Dr Linmer – are you wizards who can change the course of time itself?'

'Not wizards, not witchcraft.'

And Tam decided to tell him the truth, whatever William thought of it, for he certainly looked mystified rather than disbelieving, at the idea of another world existing some eight hundred years ahead, with a civilisation that had solved among other things the ability to move through time.

Tam also added another wonder for William: four centuries ahead there would still be ships, huge ships called liners carrying thousands of people visiting countries across the entire world.

'And in the sky, humans would fly in machines called aeroplanes like great iron birds and talk to one another in countries on opposite sides of the world. Horse-drawn carriages would give place to fast-moving machines called railway trains carrying hundreds of people and moving at speeds more than one hundred miles an hour.'

He paused for breath. William was blinking rapidly. 'Are you sure? Even the fastest horse could never achieve such speed.'

Tam continued, 'Well, I can assure you they did. There would also be machines called motor cars travelling at high speeds, which most folk, men and women, would use daily and travel from place to place in their own country and across the continents.

'But to answer your question. That world came to an end some in the year 2300 and the humans who remained moved to another planet. With all the knowledge of the past we rebuilt and moved on, discovered the secret of travelling through times past.'

'And that is how you are here in 1587,' asked William in astonishment, as he tried to assimilate all he had been told.

'Indeed, it is. We became time lords, William. We can travel back in time, but have the ability to return to our own time at the press of a button.'

'A button?'

Tam indicated his wrist.

William looked at it doubtfully. 'That is all?' He shook his head. 'This is quite beyond me.' He closed his eyes thoughtfully. 'Dr Linmer is even older than you. What happened to him?'

'Can't be sure. The poor fellow got lost.'

'Pressed the wrong button? Oh dear.' William laughed. 'Thank you for telling me all this. I want to believe you and I have my evidence from that long ago visit to my granddam at Morham that you are not an ordinary human being.' He looked at him intently and smiled. 'You both have some kind of magic. Wizards are what we would call you in our time now. However, I shall do my best and try not to believe I dreamt this conversation when I wake up tomorrow.'

It seemed to them both at that moment that a bond had been forged between the man from the past and the man from the future. However, Tam saw another immediate problem, with a solution neither of them could have dreamt of.

CHAPTER TWELVE

The Earl had received an unexpected ambassador from the young king late in the evening, who had unrolled a large map on the table between them.

He had found it difficult to concentrate on the royal command while regarding this visitor with distaste and displeasure. Bending over the map entailed being smothered by a drift of heavy perfume. Exotically dressed, painted, perfumed and arrogant, the young man was effeminate enough to be a current favourite 'gentleman of the bedchamber', if rumours regarding the monarch's preferences were to be heeded.

If Earl Robert Stewart ever took time to praise God at all, and his pious moments were rare to non-existent, it would be to thank Him for his virile sons, bred from his loins, fine strong young men. They were men in every detail like himself, his very image, virtuously turning their attentions to the charms of buxom young virgins, thrusting themselves upon them whether their attentions were wanted or not.

He frowned, for this train of thought led to Lady Marie in particular. If only she wasn't a princess and of considerable value relating to matters concerning the throne of Scotland. As such, she had been kept a virgin, or else her maidenhead would have been fought over long ago by his vigorous sons. Her purity offended him as did her virtue. It seemed unnatural as well as sad in a girl of twenty, who should have been a wife, by now possibly discarded, and a mother, unwillingly perhaps, years ago.

Well, he decided, she would return to Kirkwall with them this day, to be married by force if necessary to Patrick. With that out of the way, he would deal with the royal command from the effeminate ambassador, fluttering a lace handkerchief and holding it to his nose as if there was a bad smell. Indeed, there were many of them in the vicinity: sweating young men, dogs urinating on rugs were but a modest sample.

'His Majesty requires me to return with a progress report that the urgent matter put before you personally is now securely under way.' The Earl shuddered, thinking of the map left unrolled before him. He'd been told that the marked sites indicated possible locations where the King of Spain's gold might have been deposited, castles with access to the sea, particularly one on the north-east coast of Scotland, where a bag of Spanish gold coins had been recently found. In the matter of a treasure trove such news came the King's way. And James has been jubilant, the excitement had kept him awake at night, for he had good reason to believe this to be a fragment of the treasure.

'Aberdeenshire, did you say, it was found?' asked Patrick to his father.

The Earl responded glumly, 'His Majesty seems to think it is just across the water from Orkney.'

'Has he never looked at a map?' was the acid reply.

His father ignored that. 'It was smoothly indicated by His Majesty that you could be spared to carry on the search, as the Master of Orkney would be the most reliable person. His Majesty also hinted that a dukedom would be the reward for success.'

Patrick stiffened and said reproachfully, 'But I am to be married in the coming week, Father. This is an impossible task. It might even become dangerous.'

And as Patrick declined this royal command, his father recalled their earlier conversation when the issue had first been raised. It was the last thing Patrick wanted, to disturb the easy routine of his daily life: hunting during the hours of daylight, then eating, drinking and whoring in the evenings.

Why should any reasonable young man of noble birth with the world at his feet, wish to change such luxuries to sail out on troubled waters, have all his fine clothes ruined by getting drenched regularly in fierce storms?

Patrick had laughed, only a madman would want to exchange an easy life for such. Even a dukedom would be little recompense for the dangers of drowning.

'And who, then, is to go in search of it?' Earl Robert had demanded impatiently, having already guessed the answer that his other sons would merely laugh at him even contemplating assigning such an ignoble task to any of them.

As predicted, heads were shaken, too much trouble involved. Following Patrick's example they were fine pleased with their easy lives at home. Their shrugs of indifference had eloquently expressed that if it was a royal command and of such importance, why didn't their father, the Earl of Orkney, get all the glory by doing it himself?

Patrick was strangely silent having made it plain that he could not be expected to undertake such a hazardous task when he was about to be married. He had added virtuously, without consulting her reply, that his future bride's approval could not be expected.

The Earl regarded the landscape grimly. With Patrick out of the running, the next four brothers immediately produced reasons for declining. Everything from sore legs for such a dangerous undertaking to violent sickness when encountering sea water.

Only one remained.

'Why not give it to Owen?' Patrick demanded.

Why not indeed. His father did not miss the point. It was suddenly a brilliant idea. Owen the despised was dispensable; in fact, the brothers would all be very glad to see the last of him, if he failed to return. The Earl thought he knew the runt of his litter only too well and this suggestion fitted neatly into what he had always wanted: to rid himself and his family of his least loved son whose infirmity, that lame leg, he was ashamed of.

He smiled pleasurably. This was definitely a heaven-sent opportunity. If the plan failed and the treasure failed to appear . . . if the task was as grim and dangerous in those wild coastal seas and Owen failed to return, then neither himself nor his five brothers would regret his loss.

And so, Owen had been summoned to his father's presence. That was unusual since it was an easy matter to avoid each other in that teeming household. However, opening what Owen feared as some awkward matter, his father launched abruptly into an unexpected topic.

'We have decided that the captured pirate ship will be perfect for His Majesty's command that we locate the Spanish treasure, its presence rumoured down the coast of Scotland.' He paused, looked hard at Owen and said, 'We have not yet worked out the details but have decided that you are best able to conduct this search.'

The Earl closed his eyes, expecting to have to listen to a tirade of refusal or at best the same sullen decline he had received from his other sons. Yet much to his surprise, here was the despised and obnoxious Owen not only agreeing but even eager to take on the task.

'I am most willing, Father. I have always loved the sea and this is a fine challenge.'

The boy was actually smiling. The Earl still could not believe his ears or this sudden good fortune. At his doubtful frown, Owen hastened to remind him of what was a standing joke in the family, that even as a small boy his favourite place had not been in the comfortable surroundings of the royal court but sitting down at the cold harbour for hours, frequently in poor weather, watching the shipbuilders at work.

He said grudgingly, 'If you are successful, there will doubtless be a royal reward, perhaps even a dukedom for you. And how your brothers will envy you,' he chuckled maliciously.

He looked at Owen again. Perhaps they had been wrong about the lad. Maybe he had hidden depths. Dismissing him, he gave a contented sigh.

It would not have been so contented had he known his youngest son a little better. Or that his decision fitted in perfectly with Owen's own plan.

CHAPTER THIRTEEN

The short journey from Kirkwall Castle across to the broch was not to be delayed. It was one the Earl took rarely and always with reluctance. Today he endured it with even less enjoyment. The weather was harsh and cold, the jingle of harnesses and the trot of horses increased his headache, having overindulged in bottles of wine last night.

He had needed consolation, for it was evident that King James was commanding his immediate attention regarding the exact location and recovery of this Spanish gold. His urgency toward prompt action, even cast the urgency of Patrick's marriage into a distinctly lower category.

He turned his aching head with difficulty. Owen had asked to accompany them. His excuse was that he needed some of Baubie Finn's herbs for a favourite sick horse. What nonsense. His father had said: just shoot the beast. But Owen had refused. One of his many failings was that he loved animals.

The Earl would have rubbed his hands if they were not required to keep him on the horse. The broch would soon be on the horizon and, reining close to a silent Owen, who he hoped had not changed his mind about the mission, Earl Robert said, 'We are well pleased to have designated you this honourable task for His Majesty.'

He was left waiting for an answer, when Owen merely inclined his head, smiled and said, 'Yes, sir, I will do as you ask. I will leave immediately on His Majesty's business.'

His father uttered a wheeze of delight, still was taken aback that the delicate matter had been settled. Now there remained only the tricky business of Patrick's marriage to the royal princess Marie before he could resume his present obsession: the rebuilding and removal into the Bishops' Palace from his ruinous castle.

He glanced across at Patrick, wondering if he had heard above the jingling harnesses the content of his talk with Owen.

Patrick was silent, his thoughts far away and indifferent to royal commands. He was having his own problems, none with an easy solution. Another marriage wanted by his father only for dynastic reasons while riding alongside him was Lady Cora, who liked to pretend that she was the descendant of the Bruce, King of Scotland. She was his present mistress, a rather common woman though well-shaped enough to have netted him several years ago.

Now that he was widowed, she intended to move mistress up a notch to wife of the Master of Orkney. She had hinted that she might be pregnant and as Patrick had no children from his late marriage, she preferred not to notice that he had grown a little weary and wary of her and was more than a little bored with this longer-than-usual relationship. She looked at his sullen, withdrawn face trying to read his thoughts.

His thoughts at that moment were gloomy indeed. He was wishing he had not allowed her to come along with him. Her excuse was that she had always loved the broch after one sighting from the outside. As for Lady Marie Hepburn, she already hated her unseen, jealous of her hold over Patrick, pretend and protest as he might that this was another marriage of convenience dictated by his father and that he did not want nor was attracted by the prospect of bedding this chilly royal princess.

Lady Cora was aware that her days with Patrick were numbered. Once he was married, she would be swiftly moved on, and although she didn't care for him nor he for her, Cora was making her own plans, preparing for a bleak future and determined to have a proper place to live as compensation for enduring years in a few shabby rooms in the overcrowded palace. Not for her banishment with a small pension to some dusty old manor in Stromness, far enough away from Kirkwall and Patrick. In the forefront of her mind this day was the broch, almost but not quite a castle. Living there would suit her very well. She loved men and would have her pick of them, which had been regrettably impossible in the castle at Kirkwall.

At the beginning of her association with Patrick, she had even had a try with his father. That had been successful for a week or two, but she soon realised that the Earl did not intend her as his mistress. Her charms had more success with the other brothers, all except Owen, who had thrust her away and called her a whore.

Patrick's thoughts were on his youngest brother, riding alongside as their father reported brief details of his conversation for which he gave a sigh of relief. His easy life was no longer threatened by being forced at the King's command to go down the Scottish coast looking for some Spanish long lost gold.

As for his future bride, Marie, awaiting his arrival in the distant broch, all the signs so far had indicated a frigid, unwilling bride rather than a temporary bed of roses. Thankfully he could always ignore her and revert to other pastimes and more willing women. A final dismissive glance at Lady Cora brought rewarding thoughts of other mistresses to be had, willing and eager as well as younger and prettier by far.

From the broch's highest window, Marie and the three men, Tam, William and Linmer, listened as the jingle of harness grew louder and they warily counted numbers as the unwelcome visitors approached. The Earl had brought few servants, which indicated, as Tam had thought, that this was to be a short visit, not an overnight stay. There was only a handful of bodyguards, grim-faced, heavily built men.

'Who had never been seen to smile,' said Linmer.

There were only two of his sons and Marie's heart leapt with joy as she recognised Owen. There was only one woman, riding close to Patrick, who Marie guessed was his mistress from her elegant attire, plus a fair-sized cart.

Though she expected him this day, Marie had been warned of the Earl's imminent arrival at the broch only a short while ago, when a messenger on a fast horse rode in from Kirkwall informing them to expect the Earl within the hour 'on a progress'.

Their hearts weren't lightened by this speedy information. Panic ensued. There were problems, the least of which was that a 'progress' gave only the vaguest idea of numbers, but suggested many hungry mouths to feed and thirsty throats to quench, but with no idea of how many or for how long, it could be hours or days. In normal circumstances this invasion of even expected and welcome company took several days to prepare. Where were they to find accommodation or even, more important, the necessary food for banquets usually on demand.

Far below, growing ever closer, with the shadow of the broch above them, only Owen was pleased, his heart beating faster at the prospect of meeting Marie again. It had been so easy. His father had played into his hands, since he had a plan involving a boat and he was sure that the fisherman Halcro would willingly help Marie's escape from Orkney and the dreaded marriage to Patrick.

Owen closed his eyes, seeing a future of life happy ever after for them both waiting at Alnwick, where Lady Marie would be welcomed as a princess, the daughter of the late Queen of Scots. The Earl of Northumberland had no reason to love his counterpart in Orkney, Earl Robert, for his cruel abandonment of their daughter immediately after Owen was born and her subsequent death.

The clouds that had gathered ominously above the riders on the short journey from Kirkwall across the peninsula now burst forth.

The Earl shook a fist at the sky. Not only did his head ache but he had a very full bladder and was not impressed by the prospect before them.

'Hellish country,' he murmured, unconsoled by pleasant thoughts of fulfilling His Majesty's command and what future comforts a townhouse in Edinburgh might bring. 'Here, these warlocks and witches, should all be put to the fire and burned, the lot of them.'

As the few servants scurried about the broch kitchen far below, in terror of the Earl's anger and violence, Linmer assured them that the unwanted visitors would be bringing their own provisions.

'The Earl is aware that we have limited supplies, only what Halcro delivers each week for our needs.'

Needs that were frequently ignored as the Earl kept them as close to starvation as survival permitted.

Fortunately, Baubie was always at hand, perhaps with a secret spell, for her hens always provided eggs of a quality the Earl never encountered in his castle kitchens, as well as making nourishing soups and delicious meals assisted by Halcro's fishing, a few rabbits and the Earl's game birds. The latter would have incurred a heavy penalty had their killers been apprehended.

'What do they need that cart for, if this is only a short visit?' Marie asked.

Linmer coughed apologetically. 'Perhaps for your possessions, if they are intending you to return with them.'

She laughed bitterly. 'A small trunk would suffice for all I possess.'

This was indeed to be a brief visit, but its sinister purpose remained: to take Lady Marie unwillingly, a captive still, back to Kirkwall and marry her to Patrick.

Linmer did not give voice to this reason and, when Marie repeated the question, 'What is that cart really for?' Linmer spared her the truth.

'Plunder,' was the short reply. 'The Earl always has a cart on hand, even on the shortest visit, in case there is some item that it would be his pleasure in accepting.' In other words, carrying away any loot, large or small, that happened to take his greedy eye or that of any of his party. 'A royal prerogative,' he added mockingly.

'There is little left here he has not taken already,' said Marie.

Recognising Owen had given her reason to hope, but this was shattered immediately by the presence of Patrick.

Marie regarded the presence of Patrick's mistress ominously.

'Why has he brought her?' she whispered anxiously to Tam. He was silent.

'Just a day's outing,' William suggested.

Tam thought that unlikely and at his side Linmer murmured, 'We won't have long to wait and find out.

At any event, the Earl hates the broch. He is also scared of it. To be truthful he is scared of Baubie and the magic power he imagines she possesses – like a witch's curse. I wonder if he still has her Black Book of Arts or if he has managed to find someone to pass it on to.'

Someone shouted, 'They are here!'

They stood ready to sourly greet their unwelcome visitors as they dismounted, while William disappeared to hide in the unused upper galleries. The Earl indicated that the two guards would take care of their horses. As they approached the steps, their finery and liveries made strong contrast to their hosts.

Tam was in scholar's cloak and gown as Marie's new tutor; Linmer in a strange cloak and bonnet made by Baubie to some weird pattern long since forgotten.

Lady Marie, walking down the steps towards them, looked pale in her faded gown long out of fashion. Her wardrobe had always consisted of second- or third-hand gowns passed on by some females in the Earl's court, most likely discarded mistresses. These had been altered or remade to fit her slender frame with the help of Baubie, who numbered among her other talents that of an excellent seamstress.

Marie had inherited her mother's gift as an embroideress and was delighted when an occasional bolt of cloth unwanted at the castle had been given to her. Where gowns were concerned, she had long since ceased to care what she wore as long as it fitted, and at that moment, she cared only about how she appeared in Owen's eyes. That concerned her deeply as he bowed, holding her hand tightly and a little too long, wishing only to seize her in his arms and hold her close. She stifled a deep sigh.

Facing Patrick's bold-faced mistress, she inclined her head politely. Lady Cora did a brief curtsey, scowling meanwhile. Patrick's bride-elect was far too pretty and far too young, she thought murderously, with innocence showing up to ill-effect her own worldly-wise but rather dashed appearance, resistant to the paint and powder lavishly applied in an effort to escape the ravages of rapidly approaching middle age.

The Earl nodded to his guards, who unpacked a large barrel. 'We did not expect you to produce refreshments at such short notice.'

A breath of relief escaped from Marie. As Linmer and Tam managed respectful bows, the Earl extended a grubby hand for Marie to kiss and she said sweetly, 'Baubie Finn is happy to provide you with some of her excellent soup, Uncle Robert.'

The Earl shuddered and winced away at the suggestion of anything from that witch's cave that might add a curse to his already troubled digestive tract. 'No need for that,' was the short reply. 'We will be moving on, niece, as soon as you are in readiness to travel. We have an extra horse.'

Marie did not feel that thanks were necessary. Was the cart to transport her few household possessions? They would not take long to gather and she felt suddenly near to tears at the thought of leaving the broch. A far worse prison awaited, in an unwanted and now inescapable marriage to Patrick who, after kissing her hand, now regarded her coldly.

As they went inside the broch, Owen came to her side with a show of politeness and whispered, 'I long to be with you, Marie. I am here to see Halcro.'

He smiled for all to see and, in a whispered aside he hoped was invisible to his father, murmured, 'My business with Halcro is of deep concerns to us.'

There was no chance of further enlightenment. Marie met Halcro when he delivered their supplies from Kirkwall and she sighed inwardly, unaware of the nature of what business Owen had in mind.

Halcro was not only a fisherman. In his early days he had served as a cabin boy and later in the crew of a great galleon. Halcro had always been eager to learn and he knew all there was to know about sailing vessels.

Owen, aware of his father watching him, nodded in the direction of Baubie's cave. 'I will collect the unguents needed for the sick horse.'

'Do so, that is the reason you accompanied us,' said the Earl sharply, reminding him. He had disdainfully observed his least favourite son's cow-eyed expression in the direction of Lady Marie Hepburn. The boy was in love. How extraordinary, he thought, but she was pale and lifeless like his son and like attracted like no doubt.

The discovery of a doomed love for Owen pleased him. He chuckled to himself. Wait until he told Patrick. How his brothers would enjoy teasing and tormenting Owen on Patrick's marriage to a love that could never be his. He would just have to watch and weep, they would laugh.

As they entered the great hall, there was consternation at a cry from Lady Cora.

Zor had rushed out to meet them as he did all visitors and Cora was terrified of dogs, particularly large dogs, and this one, the size of a pony, looked like a wolf.

Clinging to Patrick's arm, she screamed in terror. 'Keep it away! Kill it!'

The guards rushed forward, swords upraised. The Earl nodded, but Linmer intercepted them with arms outstretched. 'Put your swords away, gentlemen. Zor is a family pet. He is used to welcoming visitors.'

Lady Cora continued to sob and Marie stepped between them. 'He is mine, lady, he will do you no harm.' And to the Earl, she added sternly, 'He is my only friend, uncle. Come, Zor.' He came to her side and regarded the newcomers with almost human contempt as Lady Cora clung close to Patrick's side.

Inside the hall, Mags fluttered down from her perch above the fireplace.

'Caw!' Her sudden appearance brought more screams of terror from Lady Cora.

'Kill it, Patrick, for God's sake. You know I hate birds.'

That was true. Her terror extended to any creature with fluttering wings, from tiny singing birds to the pigeons who were kept at the castle, trained to carry messages on long distances. But this was no pigeon and Patrick somewhat wearily drew out his pistol.

Again, Marie rushed forward and put a restraining hand on his arm. 'You will none of you touch Zor or Mags. They are my pets, my lord, my only friends,' she emphasised the words.

Patrick's look towards his father asked: Do I kill them to please Lady Cora? The Earl shook his head and bit his lip at all this nonsense. Lady Cora determined to be the centre of attraction.

'Oh, let them be, Patrick,' he said wearily, aware that his son would have problems enough with Lady Marie without the slaughter of her pets before her eyes. Pointing at the pistol, he said sternly, 'And put that away. Do as I tell you. They are only domestic animals, not savage beasts.'

Marie shot him a look of gratitude, the only one he received that day when he added, 'The servants will take care of them.'

Marie had another moment of panic. 'Are my servants not to accompany me?'

Even as she uttered the words, she thought of how Ina would hate living in Kirkwall and would want to return to the croft where her family lived in South Ronaldsay.

What of Linmer, though, and Baubie? She couldn't imagine Baubie being removed from her cave dwelling.

'They are to remain here. We will decide what is to happen to them later,' the Earl said, suspecting that if the plan Lady Cora had in mind was successful, the sole reason for her presence today, then once she moved into the broch, both dog and bird would suffer unfortunate accidents.

By an ironic twist of fate that was not to happen.

CHAPTER FOURTEEN

Linmer led the way across the stone floor where a table had been prepared with a few lightning food contributions from Baubie. Marie sat in the sole armchair at the head and was happy, if any could describe her as happy knowing what lay ahead for her. She was however consoled by the presence of Owen, who had slid into the seat next to her. She looked at him and he touched her hand so briefly when she longed for his lips to kiss and his arms for comfort. He smiled at her, content with her presence, even for this brief hour as she declined the Earl's wine, looking anxious and afraid and no wonder, Owen thought, longing to console her with his plan, unaware that at that moment, all her thoughts were on the fate and safety of William alias the wanted pirate Captain Morham.

Marie had been aware of hostile glances across the table from Patrick's mistress. This was now succeeded by a moan, her goblet thrust aside, as leaning against Patrick she whispered urgently in his ear.

There was a look of displeasure from both he and his father, who was making short work of the refreshments and was well into the second bottle of wine unaided. He was trying his best, and quite desperately, to raise a jolly party atmosphere in the unhappy role of an unwelcome guest. He had latched on to Tam, who had been so far unsuccessful in avoiding him and determined on introducing a somewhat drunken and slurred conversation on what life in Edinburgh did for him as a lawyer and how would it compare in exchange for Kirkwall.

Lady Cora's moans were a tiresome interruption.

'Is milady feeling unwell?' he demanded of Patrick, whose cough and miserable nod was answer enough, so turning to Marie he asked, 'Is there a chamber prepared for Lady Cora to rest a while? She is unwell.'

Marie eyed him stiffly. 'As I believe, Uncle, you are well aware, since you prepared the broch for my coming, there is no extra chamber. I have not been expected to entertain guests in my—' she was about to say 'prison', and much as she would have liked to remind him of the restrained circumstances of her life in the broch since her abduction and imprisonment for the past twelve years, she changed it to, 'only my own.'

'Then take her there to rest,' the Earl replied.

At the suggestion Lady Cora leapt to her feet. 'Come,' she said imperiously to Marie, for this was what she had been waiting for, the reason for this miserable ride from Kirkwall, a chance to look over what she had already marked down and intended as her future home. Oh, the changes she would make as well as the furnishing. That would cost the Earl a great deal of the money he was acquiring from taxing his miserable tenants to rebuild the Bishop's Palace. All around her was so dreary and dreadfully dull and cold, but she would turn it into her own palace, or a decent castle, unlike the hovel that was Kirkwall Castle, Patrick's present residence.

As for Marie, her heart was beating uncommonly fast as she led the way up the spiral stairs, slowly as possible in deference only partly to the woman she was escorting but for a more urgent reason. She was making as much noise as possible and talking loudly in what she hoped would come over as polite conversation with this unwelcome guest, all loud enough to warn William of danger and to stay in hiding.

But Cora did not notice her efforts, her mind was elsewhere as she paused occasionally, not out of breath but to give some article that interested her, large or small, careful inspection. Only once did her steps quaver and that was when she noticed Zor was following them, although remaining at a cautious distance.

'What's that wolf thing doing up here?' she cried, and Marie noticed that she no longer acted or sounded unwell and like to faint. In fact, her face had a fine glow of eagerness and excitement. 'Send it away, its presence unnerves me,' she demanded and placing her hand to her bosom, she said, 'I am like to faint.'

Marie gestured to Zor and with an almost human

nod, he sat down, but still keeping a watchful eye on them both.

'It should be in the stables. That is where animals are kept,' Cora said crossly,.

Marie replied, 'Zor goes everywhere with me. He is my guard and protector.'

This was received with an indignant sniff as the visitor returned to her careful inspections, disappointed that among the various articles there seemed little of value that even a prisoner who was also a royal princess might be expected to possess.

There were a couple of ancient tapestries, large and heavy enough to help keep out the draughts from the stone walls. They might be of value, thought Cora as she weighed their frayed edges. They would go in the Earl's cart. But no, they were very ancient and faded with their scenes of bygone battles and martyrdoms, quite hideous and depressing.

They would have to go when she moved in to be replaced by velvet hangings instead. Sad that she had found so few treasures so far, but she added the tapestries mentally to her list of changes to be made and followed up the final spiral stairs where Marie pushed open the door to her chamber. She did so quite slowly and deliberately at every step, talking very loudly, to alert William to take cover.

As Cora advanced into the room and glanced round briefly, the four-poster bed with its tapestries caught her eye. At least it looked clean and comfortable. While inspecting it, Zor had come in unseen and retreated silently to his corner where he slept at night, guarding his beloved mistress.

Still stroking the bed curtains, she dismissed the tapestries unknown to her as valuable, embroidered by Queen Mary during her long captivity and after her recent execution sent secretly to her daughter by a loyal servant. As such, they were beyond price to Marie, who indicated a garderobe and said warm water would be brought by Ina for her guest's toilet.

'You may leave us,' was the imperious response.

Summarily dismissed, Marie indignantly left to join the others in the hall.

Left alone Lady Cora did not immediately succumb to the comfort offered by the handsome carved bed, very attractive as it was. She did not realise that it had belonged to Queen Mary and such was the protocol that when kings and queens travelled, even royal travellers as prisoners, their beds went with them. The late queen's sympathisers had endeavoured to have hers restored to her daughter. Fortunately, the Earl realised neither its origins nor its significance and, considering it merely too old-fashioned, after careful inspection let it go to the broch.

Without any of this knowledge, Lady Cora continued with the part of her plan to approve the broch as her new home, promised to her by the Earl and by Patrick, when she was required to move on, instead of taking the rest she pretended to need. They had alluded that this would certainly be the case, abandoned as she would be by Patrick once he married the royal princess for political and dynastic reasons.

Her hint that she might be carrying his child had only raised the mildest of interest, but of course any offspring would, of course, be provided for and swiftly absorbed into the clan of the Orkney Stewarts.

She sighed. Having now had ample opportunity to inspect her rival, having come prepared to dislike her, she had found no reason or softer feelings to change her mind. Indifference to Patrick had been firmly settled as soon as his wife died and she became aware that there was not the least intention of her being elevated from mistress to wife of the Master of Orkney.

Walking round the handsome poster bed and testing it for comfort, she decided whatever other royal heads had slept, had loved and died on its pillows, it met with her approval and would remain here when the broch was hers.

Growing more pleased and confident, humming a little tune under her breath, she noticed for the first time the jewelled pendant hanging on the bedhead above the pillow line. This was Marie's most and only treasured possession. Having belonged to her mother it had been given to her by one of the Queen's remaining four Maries, a talisman to accompany her as she set out twelve years ago on the ill-fated voyage to meet her father Lord Bothwell in Scandinavia, ending in her abduction,

Now, Lady Cora wrenched it from its hook. Snatching it down, she did not know its sentimental value, but knew it to be an article of great worth, since here were gems, rubies, emeralds and a large sparkling diamond. She gave a little cry of delight. She would keep this, for hadn't the

Earl said she was to have any article in the broch that pleased her? Such was the rule for royal visitors, one he had himself long abided by. The cart outside had provided for the sad depletion of many a family home or castle, as well as churches the Earl had entered.

With the pendant in hand, Lady Cora looked around and saw a small looking-glass. Carrying it, she ran across to the high window for a closer examination, needing to push open the heavy shutter, a substitute covering for a window lacking glass to keep out wind and weather.

Humming under her breath, she decided to pin this new acquisition on her bonnet.

There was a movement behind her. In the excitement of her discoveries, she had forgotten all about Zor's silent presence in his corner of the room. She gave a cry of alarm as this huge animal rushed towards her.

'Shoo! Keep away—'

Circling the broch, far above, Mags was alerted to the flash of a bright stone in the now open window. She fluttered down cawing eagerly at the same moment that Lady Cora, leaning across the windowsill to escape from Zor, also fluttered down less elegantly and screaming loudly.

There was one other witness to the scene, a witness who must remain for ever silent. Exposure would cost not only his own life but that of Tam Eildor.

CHAPTER FIFTEEN

Having made his escape from the Earl and Patrick, Tam was walking in what amounted to Baubie's herb garden under the broch's sheltering walls and some thirty feet below Marie's window when it happened.

He needed time to think. This he realised was decision time, his last chance to return to his own time. Once he went to Kirkwall as Marie's tutor this would open a different and possibly very dangerous aspect on his time adventure.

The longer he stayed in Orkney, the more people he became involved with, the closer his emotional entanglement in their lives. If he disappeared, he would never know what happened to William Hepburn or Lady Marie Hepburn, since there was no mention of the Queen's daughter, only of premature twins at Lochleven, in the pages of history. As for the son of Bothwell and

Anna Throndsen, little was known of him beyond a brief reference to his childhood with his grandmother.

Tam sighed. What now? He had reached the point of no return. But could he bear to never know what happened to these new friends, return to the beach where he had landed, press the panic button? Orkney would be forgotten as another time-travel episode as he emerged centuries later in his own time. Was that the safe answer?

It might well have been so, but it was also ready too late.

There was a scream as a balloon of skirts encasing the recognisable body of Patrick's mistress hurtled down head first from Marie's window and landed almost at his feet.

He rushed forward. Lady Cora.

She was probably dead, although she had landed on soft ground. But even as he knelt down beside her, the angle of her body indicated that her neck had been broken by the fall.

Turning her over as gently as possible, he tried to place together her bare, outstretched arms and, in case there was a flicker of life, try the old method of mouth-to-mouth resuscitation.

Zor had arrived on the scene and sat watching, tail wagging eagerly, as Tam noticed the bruise on her wrist, identical to the one fast-fading on his own where the wolf-dog had dragged him from the ebb tide. Now, as Zor whined gently, Tam realised that he had tried in vain to stop her falling from the window, but his motive had been misinterpreted by the terrified woman.

'Well done, Zor,' he said. 'You did your best.'

Resuming that last hope, his desperate attempts at resuscitation, he did not hear the approach of Linmer, who had witnessed Lady Cora's death plunge, hurrying alongside the Earl and Patrick. They did not know what had occurred and, when first on the scene, were shocked speechless at the spectacle of the bent body of this man, Tam Eildor, apparently fiercely kissing Lady Cora. Their immediate thoughts were of rape.

'What is amiss?' demanded the Earl.

Tam continued to hold Lady Cora in his arms.

'Fainted or taken a fit,' said Linmer, confused, but in Tam's defence. And remembering she had complained of feeling unwell, he added. 'I will call Baubie. She will know what to do.'

'It's too late for that.' Tam spoke, for the first time aware of their approach. He stood up wearily and towered over the three men. Shading his eyes, he looked up at the window. 'The fall broke her neck. She is dead.'

Marie and Owen appeared and joined them. As the others moved aside, Tam murmured, 'She fell from your window.'

Marie gave a shocked cry. She and Owen had been alerted by Zor's odd behaviour, his strange movements, rushing up and down the staircase and then out of the door and in again. Linmer had been unaware that there was something wrong, as sitting nearby he had been trying hard to overhear what he gathered was a conspiratorial conversation between the Earl and Patrick over a fresh bottle of wine.

Hovering near the body, all continued to regard Tam enigmatically while awaiting some further explanation. The Earl showed no desire for a closer look and had retreated to a safe distance.

Tam regarded the silent Patrick, who had not made any sign of emotion, such as the cry of anguish and disbelief that Tam would have expected of any man losing his lover in such circumstances.

'Are you certain?' asked the Earl, eyeing him coldly.

'The lady is dead. She fell from the window up yonder. None could have survived such a fall.'

Tam looked up, remembering the shadow he had seen. 'There is nothing more we can do.' Without awaiting further comment, he moved quickly to the door of the broch. The speed at which he moved, more like flying than walking on solid ground, always took Linmer by surprise.

In this instance he knew the reason for Tam's urgency: to reach that upstairs room. The Earl and Patrick must not discover Captain Morham alias William Hepburn in hiding.

As Tam entered the building, the picture of the Earl and Patrick remained frozen in his mind, the fact that both looked unconcerned. Would he ever forget such stony, unemotional faces, such a dire reaction to the dreadful scene he had left? It was as though the dead body belonged to an animal, a person unknown, a nameless servant, not to a woman who had lived in intimacy with Patrick and had been part of the Earl's unacknowledged family in Kirkwall Castle for several years.

Tam was appalled. Was that how the aristocracy lived in the sixteenth century, seeing violent death as an everyday experience? He would have been even more surprised if he could have seen into the heads of those two men who had known Lady Cora best.

In addition to their private reasons for relief rather than grief at Lady Cora's untimely end and no stranger to witnessing violent death, regrettably often at his own hands, the Earl was aware that certain immediate procedures were to be followed.

The speedy removal of Lady Cora's body from the scene was the utmost priority. Next, was how this unfortunate event could be twisted to his own advantage. Her hints and nudges had more than indicated that she was with child. The Earl was displeased but not shocked. It was by no means unique for the mistress of one of his sons, legitimate or bastard, living under the castle's leaking roof to find herself in a similar condition.

The solutions were varied, and his knowledge and advice rarely involved in providing one. The quest for a solution in Lady Cora's situation, her need for air and a chance to explore the broch as her future residence, had taken care of that urgent matter and had cost her her life.

Taking Patrick aside, to a casual bystander his silence and lack of emotion might have been taken as the shocked grief of a bereaved lover for his adored mistress, but the Earl knew his son all too well for that. What little conscience Patrick had was not striking him.

'What think you of matters?' demanded his father.

Patrick sighed. He had long since wearied of Cora. She

had a vile temper and, since his forthcoming marriage to Lady Marie promised little in the way of comfort, he was already making a list of certain other younger, prettier ladies in the court, who would be willing and grateful to step into his now deceased mistress's shoes.

He shrugged. 'God's will, one must suppose,' was his pious response to his father's vague question. God had certainly come up with the perfect solution.

'Her body must be moved from here,' said the Earl.

Mistresses being moved on but by less disastrous means was a familiar situation over the years and it did not bother him in the least, but a dead one, perhaps murdered, was another matter entirely.

'Fortunately, we have the cart,' he said, and was rewarded by a sour look from Patrick, who was seeing nothing but trouble and personal inconvenience looming on the horizon.

His father was wearing the frown that indicated serious thought.

Having seen Tam Eildor in that passionate display over Cora's body and declaring that he had found her lying there, suggested that if this could be proved as murder, here was the perfect suspect.

Eildor could be incriminated, put on trial and executed. Elimination was the perfect solution. There was something odd and rather frightening about this man who had failed to be the spy the Earl had hoped for. The thought of getting rid of him permanently had instant appeal.

His hoped-for suspect was at that moment surveying the open window, some thirty feet above their heads, with Zor at his side. The Earl saw them move, eyed him thoughtfully and quickly turned his attention to Patrick, who hovered uncertainly, biting his lip.

'You must take the body back to Kirkwall. Master Eildor will return with you and see that he writes down a statement, the details of all that happened, how he happened to be in the vicinity when she fell,' the Earl added ominously, stroking his chin thoughtfully. 'Meanwhile we will look into matters, before joining you with Dr Linmer and Lady Marie. Lady Marie will remain here at the broch until a legal conclusion is reached. We may have to delay the wedding . . .'

In answer Patrick frowned darkly. 'How are we to transport her? We have no coach.'

'We have the cart and that will be adequate..'

Before more questions could be asked, he hurried inside the broch where Linmer, Owen and Marie were waiting in the great chamber. The lady's tearful reaction was the most emotion so far displayed.

'Oh, the poor lady, how terrible!'

Regarding Marie's servant and the other two maids who had been wrapping the corpse into what most resembled a large untidy parcel, he looked at the group, the sad faces, and said, 'Be seated.'

Tam had left them with a feeling of deep unease when he ran up the staircase to Marie's room. Perhaps this was the moment for his return to his own time. Just walk out and leave them to it, walk down to the beach. It was so easy. But no, he had to see the outcome of this mystery

140

especially as it involved the future of Marie and Owen.

He had to be the first on the scene of Cora's accident in case William was trapped, still in hiding there. The door was open.

He called a tentative, 'William?' There was no reply. The room was empty. He looked around. What did he expect to find?

There was very little in the way of evidence apart from a smashed looking-glass beside the open window, indicating that Cora had found something small and taken it over to the window for a closer look, but leaning out where the light was better had overbalanced.

Zor was at his heels, having followed him up the staircase, and was now by the window, looking first at Tam and then staring down with an almost human expression of anxiety.

'If only you could talk,' Tam said wearily, wondering if science in his own time might one day be able to give animals speech humans could understand.

Anxious to prevent any search for evidence that would reveal Captain Morham in hiding, he stroked Zor's head and whispered, 'If Lady Cora was feeling faint, as would seem most likely, we must presume she leant out too far and, despite your grip on her wrist, she lost balance and fell.'

Again, he called, 'William?', but there was no response.

Yet there was another possibility for the accident, Tam thought, as he remembered seeing a shadow as he bent over her body far below. Had she seen this stranger, then panicked and fallen? That suggested she was at the window for some guilty reason. Tam leant out but there was nothing to see. The only indication of something amiss was Zor's odd behaviour, his frantic running to the poster bed and back again to the window.

At that moment, he heard footsteps as Marie appeared, with Mags fluttering on her shoulder.

She stroked the bird's head. 'She was trying to tell me something, Tam, going back and forth to her perch. You will never guess what I found there,' she continued indignantly, 'my mother's jewelled pendant!' She pointing to the bed. 'From the headboard over there. It was very firmly fixed years ago and couldn't be removed except by lifting it off the hook. Mags could never have done that. Besides she would never take any shining jewel, however tempting, that belonged to me. 'Would you, my darling?' she ended.

She was rewarded by a gentle 'Caw.'

For Tam, a picture was forming. A solution to the mystery. Cora had removed the pendant and her action was observed by Zor. But Cora, terrified of dogs, had tried to shoo the huge animal away and ran to the window still clutching the pendant. Zor had seen she was in danger and tried to save her, hence the identical bruise on her wrist to the now fading one on Tam's own.

The scene at the window had been witnessed by Mags and, always fascinated by the glitter of a diamond, she had spotted the jewel that the woman was trying to fix to her bonnet and had swooped down for a closer look. Also terrified of birds, Cora had tried to shoo both creatures away, especially the magpie which appeared to be darting straight at her head, cawing loudly.

'That's the answer to the mystery,' Tam said to Marie. 'No human agency pushed Lady Cora out of the window. Zor and Mags were responsible for her death. They were her killers.'

'And her own greed, stealing my mother's jewel,' Marie replied. 'I hope God will forgive her, but now I realise that she came to the broch for one purpose only: to claim it once I went to Kirkwall and married Patrick.

'In the interval,' Marie added indignantly, 'she decided to steal whatever took her fancy. She knew that was in accordance with the Earl's rule on royal visits, one might take whatever pleased, and I saw her making notes, especially of a couple of tapestries that I am fond of, embroidered by my mother during the long years of her captivity. I treasured them, but the pendant most of all.'

She sobbed. 'I could forgive anything but that.' Wiping her eyes, she shivered and listened quietly to the sounds of busy activity. 'It is God's just punishment for an evil deed,' she whispered, 'that it is herself and not my tapestries to be loaded on to the cart and carried back to Kirkwall.'

The sound of footsteps announced the arrival of William, who had been hiding in an upper gallery turret. 'I saw what happened. I could have saved her, but I was too late.' His account was exactly what Tam had worked out. 'I tried to seize her. The dog was hanging onto her wrist, I rushed forward but seeing me, a stranger, made matters even worse. She cried out, struggled despite Zor's grip and fell.' He sighed. 'I could only stand by and watch.'

'And you are the only witness, a witness unfortunately who cannot come forward and reveal the truth . . .'

'Without revealing the existence of the wanted Captain Morham,' Tam added grimly.

CHAPTER SIXTEEN

In the hall below the Earl was himself again, revelling in his powers of life and death. Here was a situation that could be worked to his advantage.

Patrick had been despatched with Lady Cora's body to the mortuary at Kirkwall until his father had assembled a court of law. With a case of murder that his prearranged jury would accept. That was in their best interests or rather the judges' best interests, since they dared not do otherwise.

The verdict would be that Lady Cora had been foully murdered, pushed to her death by none other than the man they found bending over her. Master Tam Eildor would be put on trial and condemned to death. Such a happy, easy solution.

Tam's friends were horrified.

When they realised that the Earl's intentions included

the castle dungeons rather than a mere statement of having witnessed Lady Cora's fall, Marie in particular said, 'Why Tam? He only found her. Surely, I was the most likely suspect, seeing that she had come to my home, thinking it already hers once I was married off. Meanwhile she was stealing from me—'

'Since you were with the doctor and I when it happened, that is not a possibility,' said Owen, laying a hand on her arm.

As far as Marie was concerned, that was thankfully true, but there would be no mention of the tapestries or the jewelled pendant, the greed which had cost Lady Cora her life. Nor of her real killers, Zor and Mags. And the known fact that she was afraid of dogs and birds and might have overbalanced in her attempts to escape from them would be disregarded.

These important details would not appear, erased from whatever evidence was provided. The murderer, the man appearing on trial, in front of the regulated, carefully instructed jury, was Tam Eildor, who would be condemned by an overwhelming verdict. Determined to keep him under close scrutiny, the Earl had already decided to remove him to Kirkwall immediately and put him in close confinement until the trial could be arranged.

Such was law in Earl Robert Stewart's reign, and this was not the first time an innocent man or woman had been condemned simply because the verdict suited a whim of the Earl or, more important, access to their property which automatically reverted to the state.

Patrick was not best pleased that he was to be in charge of Master Eildor on the short journey back to the castle. Truth to tell, the presence of this man made him very uneasy. He did not like things or persons he could not understand and the strange new tutor fitted the role uncommonly well.

When he grumbled to his father, the Earl said, to his disgust, 'You can use his help with the necessary arrangements at the mortuary and the funeral.'

Patrick frowned. The funeral was to be a big problem as little or nothing was known of Cora's family, if she had one, apart from her claim to King Robert the Bruce, the truth of which was difficult to verify.

Arrangements were made for an immediate return to Kirkwall and a very uneasy Tam was to accompany them. He had no option in the matter. He thought grimly that he should have touched that panic button before being firmly seized by the two grim guards and padlocked into the cart beside Lady Cora's shrouded corpse.

He looked helplessly across at Marie and Owen. Panic seized him, as he mouthed the words, 'What of William?'

He whispered this question to Linmer, who hovered anxiously nearby overseeing the arrangements for departure, grateful that Marie was to stay at the broch meantime.

'Halcro will take care of him,' he murmured.

'Halcro?'

Linmer gave a confident nod. It appeared that Baubie's husband, mostly ignored, was not just the simple fisherman but a figure of importance in the community. He had contacts among the seafaring men and would arrange for William to get back to his ship at that moment securely disguised as a merchant vessel resting at the dock in Kirkwall harbour.

'He will be quite safe.'

The Earl's party mounted and prepared to leave with Tam, a reluctant and somewhat agitated prisoner. But even if he were free to reach the beach and make his exit from this time, he knew this was not the opportune moment for his escape, although this would have been the perfect solution. What about those he left to dance to the Earl's deadly music?

His sudden terrifying and unexplainable disappearance would be classed as witchcraft. Linmer, Marie and her servants, as well as Baubie Finn, regarded an excuse to set the fires burning in the marketplace of Kirkwall.

There was only one unfortunate impediment to Halcro's plan, Tam thought, as the Earl's party began their exit from the broch. One of the Earl's guards, more adventurous than the others and the possessor of a curious disposition, had long been intrigued by the non-existent history of the broch and had decided to take this unique opportunity where he might not be missed for a few moments to explore the upper galleries of the broch. There, much to his surprise, he had encountered none other than the notorious and badly wanted pirate captain whom he recognised immediately, even without the beard, by his distinctive russet curls.

He drew out his pistol ready for an easy capture since the escaped prisoner carried no firearms, but William was badly shaken at his own folly, the victim of his own curiosity and should have remained in hiding, instead of coming to the battlements to see what was happening far below.

The guard, whose name was of no importance, to the Earl led his captive down and handed him over with an air of triumph, delightedly envisaging the prospect of that rich reward for single-handedly capturing this wanted man.

He was somewhat taken aback trying to splutter it all out, his bravery and so forth, by the Earl's preoccupied look. Expecting to be praised, his courage applauded, the captain placed in chains and returned to prison in Kirkwall to await his overdue hanging, the Earl was indulging in one of his long-drawn frowns as he regarded William and had to search for a much faster than normal bout of face-saving.

To the waiting assembly, he said, 'We have matters to discuss. Come with me.' He seized William, watched by an open-mouthed guard, who saw his captive being hustled out of sight and his dreamt-of reward vanishing like fairy gold.

Meanwhile, anticipating what he dared not think, William followed the Earl back inside the broch where, without preliminaries, in a few words, he was launched into the business of his son, Owen Stewart, a royal command concerning Spanish treasure and the necessity of immediately finding a captain for his own ship, the *Falcon* now under close guard.

The Earl had stopped speaking. A moment later, William was being offered a choice. Be willing to take charge of this assignment or, under sentence of death, be hanged as a pirate tomorrow.

Would he be willing? Of course, there was no guarantee, but since they had little evidence of his privateering in Orkney waters, the Earl was confiding the difficulties that might be expected in proving a case against him, without also revealing evidence of the island's profitable wrecking activities.

It was all bewildering to William, who at last got the gist of what the Earl was saying. He wasn't to hang after all. He was to take command of his own ship again and go on a mission for His Majesty King James regarding some obscure treasure, its exact whereabouts unknown but rumoured to be in a castle on the north-east coast of Scotland. This, said the Earl with a gesture of dismissal, was a task for which Captain Morham was admirably well suited, since he was familiar with the waters of that region from his less lawful activities. William decided to ask a favour, seeing as he was momentarily in the Earl's good books.

'Sir, may I remain in the broch until tomorrow?'

The Earl's eyes narrowed, expecting treachery, until William smiled. 'I have just met my half-sister, Lady Marie, and would like to spend a little time with her. This is our first meeting. Our father was Lord Bothwell, as I expect you know.'

The Earl had not associated Captain Morham with being Bothwell's son and Marie's half-brother;

indeed, he was also related to William. It gave him confidence in the treasure-seeking enterprise and he granted the request. One never knew when such a link with royal connections might prove useful.

CHAPTER SEVENTEEN

The Earl's departure from the broch with Tam in their midst had been watched with dismay and Owen, riding alongside the cart, tried to convey reassurance to Tam with a nod. He was unable to take it further, that Tam's imprisonment and trial were the main reason for himself leaving a somewhat distraught Marie, whose only consolation was that she was not riding with them to marry Patrick.

With only the jingle of harnesses, the cart firmly watched over and the safety of its contents anxiously regarded, they reached Kirkwall without further alarms and in blessedly fair weather ornamented by birdsong.

Tam was wondering what close confinement would mean and again plagued with the certainty that he had left his place of safe return behind at the broch.

It was a short journey. When Kirkwall Castle

emerged from the dying light, he was pushed without ceremony down a steep spiral staircase into what looked remarkably like a well-used dungeon. Evil-smelling, dark and cold, it gave Tam more cause for unease, regardless of Owen's indication that all would be well.

Darkness increased and so did the silence. After an anxious hour or so, without any provision of food or water, he heard heavy footsteps and recognised Owen's voice, sharply informing the guard that the prisoner was to be placed in his custody. The son of the Earl with a stern authoritarian manner gave the guard no valid reason for argument.

The door was opened and Owen somewhat unceremoniously seized Tam's arm, making the scene look remarkably less like a rescue than an approaching trial. Impressed by Owen's performance, Tam would not have cared to exchange places with any prisoner in the custody of one of the Earl's sons, since, according to what was ugly gossip among the guards, they were not beyond a bit of torture as an evening's entertainment.

Once outside, Tam's knees had ceased to tremble, and with Owen's strong grip on his arm released, he sighed with relief, thanking him for having so speedily come to his rescue.

Owen laughed. 'The Earl's sons fortunately don't have to give reasons or produce warrants, but what I intend now is to get us onto William's ship and away from Kirkwall with all possible speed. First, we must go to the broch and collect Marie and the doctor. I have horses ready.'

As they walked towards the stables, Tam asked, 'What will your father do when he finds I am not there to be put on trial?'

Owen smiled. 'I have told him that I wish to have you as crew on the ship, that you have some valuable knowledge regarding finding treasures and such matters.'

It seemed a feeble excuse. Although losing the chance of a trial, Owen was aware that his father had seemed somewhat relieved, since he uneasily believed that this Tam Eildor might have unusual skills and as such should be invaluable in locating the treasure. In any case, the Earl wanted rid of this Tam Eildor, who scared him and left him with a sickening a sense of doom. He avoided those strange, luminous eyes that seemed to look through him and, a believer in witchcraft, he was sure that Eildor might put a curse upon him. He had enough to contend with these days, in the natural world, without inviting disasters from the unknown.

He was to remember his last words to Owen when he had sternly advised his youngest son that he would be exceedingly displeased if Eildor ever set foot in Orkney again. Without spelling it out in as many words, he indicated that he was relying on Owen to get rid of him on the return voyage, once their mission was accomplished.

'That should not be a problem on a ship. A man falling overboard is an easy accident to arrange.' Then with a rare moment of confidence, the Earl added, 'As long as I never set eyes on him, I shall be content,' then handed Owen a document to be put directly into His Majesty's hands.

'Captain Morham will take command. He should be glad that we are giving it to him, instead of the hanging as he deserves. I shall put some of our own trusted sailors as crew. They will obey your orders as my son and you will be in charge of the mission.'

Owen wryly remembered his father's final words. 'Once you have reached your destination and hopefully found the treasure, you may do whatever you wish with our pirate captain. He must also disappear. Hang him if you like.'

So, Owen parted company with his father, whose sentiments of hoping never to meet again they shared. Owen had the additional intention of never setting foot in Orkney again, for the main purpose of his voyage on the *Falcon* was a step on the way to seeing himself and Marie married and living happily in Northumberland.

Returning to the broch with Tam, Owen's account delighted his friends as they realised that the Earl had fallen into what might be described as a God–given trap.

They sat around the table in what passed as the great hall and were joined by Baubie, who had cleared the untidy debris of a meal left by the Earl's visit. As she replaced their settings with nourishing plates of something extremely delicious with contents vaguely meaty, but of an unknown origin, Tam was reassured by Halcro whispering that it was one of her favourite recipes.

Owen took his place at the head of the table and related the conversation with his father.

William then stood up and gave an account of his weird interview with the Earl, who had told him that instead of being hanged next day as he had expected, he would be captaining the *Falcon* as part of His Majesty's treasure-seeking command.

'I could hardly believe my ears,' William said. 'Being free again. That blessed relief.'

Owen knew they must join the ship immediately in case the Earl discovered how his decision fitted neatly in with Owen's own plan. 'Finding a captain would have been a problem, without revealing that we had him already. With no idea until then what my father had in mind, I could only think of many devious explanations as to why we were giving an escaped pirate sanctuary refuge in the broch.'

He spread his arms wide. 'But see how it has worked out so splendidly and we owe a debt of gratitude to that guard's unearthing him, having him returned to the castle dungeon where I was in the fortunate position of being able to have him released into my custody.'

The listeners shared his laughter and relief, particularly Marie, who leant over and took her half-brother's hand.

What next? That was the question. What was their next move? What had Owen in mind?

'I don't trust a crew signed on by your father,' William said. 'Halcro will gather men for us. He has the experience and knows who to trust in the seafaring community.'

There were nods of agreement as Owen said, 'My father's decision also fits with the unfortunate events regarding Lady Cora's demise. Patrick will now be deeply involved in matters relating to her funeral, unlikely to be straightforward by any stretch of imagination or easy to arrange since none of us at court, least of all Philip, knew of any family. She was always deliberately vague except to boast about the supposed Bruce connection.'

They were to learn later of a connection with Tankerness House in Kirkwall, that she had been a servant there and arrangements suitably financed were to be set in store for her funeral.

'It may take some weeks, with any thoughts of marriage postponed,' Owen added with a relieved smile at Marie. 'That is in our favour. By the time it is resolved, I hope we will all be clear of Orkney for ever.'

Reaching out with a tender glance, Marie grasped his hand.

But what was going to happen to her meantime?

Owen went on, 'The delayed marriage is to our advantage. Time is on our side.'

Heads were shaken. Not only Tam's, who now had serious misgivings about the reliability of time. Anxious looks were exchanged. No one cared for the idea of leaving Marie at the broch, but Owen rubbed his hands together and laughed.

'Don't you see? We will take Marie with us.'

Marie sighed gratefully at the thought of not being parted from Owen. She would be happy to follow him to the world's end 'clad in only a petticoat', as her mother had once said of her love for Lord Bothwell.

She could see that the others seated round the table had their doubts about Owen's idea of taking her on the voyage with them.

Glances were directed across at William. What would be his reaction? As captain of a pirate ship in particular he knew that sailors regarded the presence of a woman on board brought ill luck, but he merely smiled at her.

'I shall always look to my sister's safety and well-being. My relief at her escape from a dreadful marriage is beyond words. And I have no objections to her sailing with us.'

'And how do we intend to manage that, sir?' Linmer asked.

Owen had the answer. 'You must all have observed her servant Ina.' He paused and whispered, 'If you haven't, look now. Don't you see what I'm intending?'

They looked and turned again to him, the idea dawning of what he had in mind.

'You don't mean that Ina should impersonate Marie?'

Owen smiled and shook his head. No, that was impossible, seeing that Ina was taller, more heavily built and would have been difficult for anyone to accept as the slender twenty-year-old princess.

'Not Ina, Nan.' He pointed towards another servant Marie was allowed, Ina's young cousin helping Baubie clear the table of the remaining dishes. 'Don't you see, Nan and Marie are the same height and roughly the same age.' Pausing, he looked at Marie and said, 'Fortunately Nan shares your height and you are both the same slender shape – perfect material for a disguise.'

'A disguise?' murmured Marie.

Owen grasped her hand again. 'Yes, my dearest. Nan will take your place here in the broch while you become a cabin boy on Captain Morham's ship, wearing boys' clothes until we are safely out at sea well past Kirkwall. Then you can become a lady again as we hunt for the King's treasure trove.'

It was Marie's turn to clasp her hands together and laugh in delight. This was such an exciting prospect being at Owen's side, she believed she could face any danger. Nothing in this world she imagined could be worse than being married to the Master of Orkney. And she would enjoy her life as a cabin boy. It touched remembrance of tales about her gallant, fearless mother.

How the Queen, wearing boys' clothes borrowed from courtiers, escaped from the confines of Holyroodhouse at night to roam the streets of Edinburgh and visit taverns. She enjoyed sitting down with a tankard of ale, regarding this as the rightful opportunity for a monarch to mingle unrecognised and learn from ordinary citizens the way they believed a kingdom should be ruled.

'Such an adventure, such happy times. She loved life,' Marie said to Owen, tearful at how it had all ended for her mother.

Listening and saying little, Tam realised this was another moment of decision, his chance perhaps to watch them leave on that mighty sea voyage and return to his own time. But even as the thought struck him, he knew again he could never do it. Here was a chance to experience yet another aspect of this sixteenth century world, in an era he would never have chosen again. He had been captivated and enchanted by the strange beauty of Orkney and grown close to the broch, to Lady Marie and her half-brother, William Hepburn, Dr Erasmus Linmer, Baubie Finn, as well as Zor.

He was now a part of their lives and cared deeply what might happen on the *Falcon*, although he had could not recall ever having any desire to sail anywhere, after reading horrid tales from Planet Earth about seasickness. How those who suffered moaned that death would be too good. But surely, they were misquoted? Sailing away from Orkney, always within sight of the east coast of Scotland, would present no great oceans to cross.

And now there was the possibility of visiting Edinburgh. Oh, what a chance to see the city in 1587. This was an adventure he was not willing to miss.

He looked at Linmer in quiet conversation with William, who was about to return to Kirkwall and make the final arrangements for sailing. The doctor had said nothing so far to contribute to Owen's plan.

'Have you ever been to sea, doctor?'

Linmer shook his head. 'Not that I remember, but I am willing to give it a try.'

He sounded suddenly weary. 'I have long been an alchemist. I have no other memories now of what was my life before. But I still have my curiosity – as to what will become of this madness of a treasure trail – and that has overcome an old man's thoughts of safety.'

Around him the plans were being discussed with William, how they could best be put into effect. Owen was again stressing a sense of urgency, that it must be done speedily.

How was Marie to escape? She said, 'I can hardly go into Kirkwall with my pets and join William's ship with you Owen. Even in boys' clothes, Uncle Robert has sharp eyes, he is aware that Tam and the doctor were coming from the broch and that I was to remain there for the present until Patrick was ready for our marriage.'

Tam observed her bewilderment and asked Owen, who had convinced them of his efficiency as an organiser by putting forward so many smart ideas.

Halcro had joined them round the table and, leaning forward, he said, 'You leave that to me, Lady Marie. I go out with my fishing boat every day and once the *Falcon* is under way and past the harbour control at Kirkwall, I will row out back to the broch here, collect you in rowing boat and deliver you to the ship at anchor a mile or so out to sea.' He turned to William. 'I have engaged a crew, all reliable honest Orkney men.'

That solution brought relief, and though William had said the least, he looked happiest. Tam realised that the captain was delighted at the prospect of commanding his ship again, but there was more than that.

William had a secret plan of his own that he had admitted to no one, not even his beloved half-sister. He intended to make anchor off the Mearns on the Aberdeenshire coast, where he would ride up the hill and visit his beloved Susannah in Muchalls Tower. He did, however, have one urgent and more practical problem.

'The *Falcon* needs a pilot.'

And they remembered that the pilot, who had also been captured and had escaped with Owen's help at the same time as William, had taken this golden opportunity to disappear from Orkney.

All heads turned hopefully towards Owen

Owen knew much about ships thanks to a lifetime's occupation of watching those shipbuilders at work, but he shook his head sadly. Building ships did not include how to sail them.

'It is no cause for concern.'

Again, it was Halcro who had been listening to the conversation that announced this. 'If Captain Morham is agreeable, I will be your pilot and your boson.' They all looked at him. Far from being simply the fisherman at the broch and, still to Tam's amazement, Baubie Finn's husband, Halcro had other hidden depths.

They listened eagerly as he told them how he had served in his early days, like William, as a cabin boy on a great ship, a fighting man o' war. He knew all about ships, had a long-sustained interest in them, great and small, sails, depths and maps. He was delighted at the prospect of joining what he imagined to be a splendid but dangerous adventure of treasure-seeking away from his daily routine on Orkney for a while.

Perhaps that was the solution for Tam. Halcro had solved his most pressing problem and would get him back to the beach at the broch, his return ticket to the year 2300.

'Well done.' With a grin William slapped Halcro's shoulder. 'We have one part of our treasure found already,' he said. He turned to the others. 'As well as a captain and a boson, we now have ready all the necessary ingredients for a sailing ship.'

It was decided. Owen would be their leader in this enterprise as he also had the advantage of being regarded by the seamen as a cut above the notorious Stewarts. He had established good terms with the ordinary folk of Kirkwall, men who had watched him grow up and realised that even as a wee lad, and son of the hated Earl, he was not in the least like his wicked brothers.

They felt they could trust him and, on his side, Owen was certain that the crew Halcro had chosen would obey William's command, especially as they went in fear of sea law recrimination, which would be hanging if they disobeyed their captain.

And so the arrangements were swiftly made, with Marie joining the *Falcon* as cabin boy, leaving in the broch a servant near to her in shape and size and wearing her clothes.

Nan had been taken aback, honoured and delighted, although afraid that on close contact she certainly could never behave like the young princess.

Marie had laughed. 'That should not be too difficult. I have never prided myself on behaving like royalty since I had little exposure to how they behaved before I left Scotland when I was eight.'

As Marie gave her final instructions, Baubie Finn would be taking care of matters within the broch and as cook and housekeeper taking good care that none discovered Lady Marie's secret and her maid's substitution. Should the Earl wish to speak to Marie or, worst of all but also most unlikely, should appear in person, he would be informed by Baubie, since the Earl was unable to read sign language of the mute Ina, that yes, she was in her room in the upper gallery but had a high fever which might be infectious. Nan would then appear at the high window, if the Earl insisted, but far enough away to be convincing in Marie's gown and headdress.

During the following days, Tam and Linmer joined William at the steering wheel of his ship. Now the sails were set, all ready and awaiting the next tide for their departure, when the Earl suddenly appeared. Panic-stricken, they watched his arrival only to be informed he was here merely to look the ship over and see that all was in order.

The *Falcon* was a frigate, a three-masted, full-rigged sailing ship now flying the Scottish ensign, the colours of the King of Scotland that the Earl considered would bring the respect and reverence of any given vessels it encountered on the voyage down the north-east coast. She was ready to ship anchor and leave, slipping out of Kirkwall harbour on the outgoing tide.

Patrick had rode to the harbour, but declined to join his father's inspection. The crew were lined up to be solemnly looked over, while he asked questions relating to their quarters and generally seemed interested, an attitude in his case, which William and Owen interpreted as one of uncertainty and suspicion.

Watching him with disquiet, the three men drew deep breaths that the original plan had been abandoned and Marie in her cabin boy's disguise was not with them.

Fortunately, the Earl did not know or care enough about ships to observe anything untoward. Preparing to disembark, he cast one last nervous glance across at Tam Eildor, who was staring steadily ahead. He was glad to see this weird man go. If all went according to his instructions to Owen, then he would never see him or the erstwhile pirate again.

Watching as the ship bobbed out of sight into the waters beyond Kirkwall, the Earl and Patrick turned their horses back up the road to the castle, both silently busy with their own thoughts.

For those on the *Falcon*, the moment of launching then observing the entourage of the Earl and Patrick growing smaller and smaller, finally diminishing altogether as the ship crossed the harbour into the ocean, caused them all to breathe freely again. They had shared uneasy feelings that this had been all too simple and feared a last-minute change of heart from the Earl.

William's second thoughts regarding the success of the mission were manifold but useless, considering the ship's destination, a mere spot on the map the King had left with Owen. This was a hastily drawn copy depicting an improbable and isolated castle down the coast a few miles from Edinburgh. The fact that it was owned by one Robert Logan, a man with a reputation only a little less savoury than the Earl's, did little for his peace of mind.

The castle itself shared an unsavoury reputation, a haunt of smugglers and spies from France, although it had seen occasional notable and even royal visitors, including the late Queen, who had stopped off on occasion en route for some other destination. That did not concern the King, however, who was notable for a lack of caring or even interest in his mother. All that concerned him most urgently were rumours that had drifted into Edinburgh of the treasure having been possibly deposited at Fast Castle.

He had given that considerable thought and decided that now the Earl Robert Stewart of Orkney, the Queen's half-brother and His Majesty's half-uncle by bastardy, would impress Robert Logan and make a splendid screen to hide behind rather than declare himself as an anxious treasure-seeker.

For this purpose of creating a good impression, the *Falcon* also carried gifts of wine, honey and other luxury items such as suitable foodstuffs for an isolated castle on a clifftop.

Back in the Kirkwall Castle courtyard, the Earl dismounted. The plan was in action, the next step was to inform King James that his command had been obeyed and a ship, the *Falcon*, was on its way to pick up the treasure indicated and to deliver it, by his youngest son, Owen, personally into His Majesty's eagerly waiting hands. The royal mission accomplished, Robert Stewart, Earl of Orkney, would await a suitable and hopefully generous reward.

Climbing the steep stairs into the great presence chamber where he worked, still the scene of untidy table and discarded maps, among his neglected plans for the Bishop's Palace, he was gnawed by his first misgivings.

Had he done the right thing, and most importantly, was Captain Morham to be trusted? The Earl was relying on his past privateering activities and, though he had seemed eager and more than willing, that could have another, more sinister interpretation, that the pirate was merely glad to have his ship returned to him, the treasure mission of scant consideration. Of course, Owen was in charge and would keep a stern eye on everyone, whatever their differences in the past. So what was he worrying about? Then he realised the nugget of fear at the back of his mind that refused to be dissolved: the presence on that expedition of Tam Eildor, a man or wizard to be feared.

At his side Patrick was preoccupied and had ignored or failed to hear his father's complaints and uncertainties. Untroubled by that delayed marriage he had plans for a new mistress, a very shapely girl he had met, who seemed, or so he fancied, not be unwilling to take Cora's place.

The Earl, however, interpreted his silence as being disagreeably involved in what lay immediately ahead, arranging the funeral of Lady Cora as speedily and as cheaply as possible from his meagre allowance, always providing he could track down some of her relatives to meet the expense. His thoughts turned to Tankerness House. He suspected that she had connections there and it would make a start, especially as he had seen her in conversation with a girl whose dark complexion hinted at wilder shores than Orkney's pale skins.

When questioned, Cora had laughed. The girl was only a servant, a slave of some sort. She knew nothing about her except that she was an excellent seamstress.

'Her name?'

Cora had shrugged. Such things were of little importance.

'Juna, I think.'

CHAPTER EIGHTEEN

The day before their departure had been wrapped in a confusion of incidents for Tam.

His last sight of Kirkwall was one he would not forget as Halcro's rowing boat approached the anchored ship having collected Lady Marie with her hastily wrapped bundle of clothes from the broch.

The overhanging, slightly swaying vessel well above her head, Marie climbed the rope ladder lithe as a seasoned sailor, in her new guise as cabin boy. Tam lent her a hand as she clambered aboard and congratulated her. 'Well done, you did that as if you joined ships at sea every day of your life.'

She laughed delightedly. 'Do I not make a fine boy?' She was enjoying her new experience of wearing boys' clothes and Tam saw that she was not alone.

'What about him?' he asked, watching as Zor was hauled aboard.

'Did you not see him?' Marie asked. 'There wasn't room for him, far too big for a rowing boat, so he just swam alongside.'

As Tam followed her to where William was waiting to give the order to raise the anchor, her slim, boyish shape that Patrick had so despised helped her to make a convincing cabin boy, where curves and a large bosom would have given the game away.

He shuddered, remembering the accident, wondering how Patrick was coping with the funeral arrangements.

He thrust that aside; there were other memories too.

Tam thought of his last words with Ina's young cousin, Nan, dressed as Lady Marie and ready to take her place at a distance. What if the Earl and Patrick arrived without warning to find that Marie had fled on the *Falcon* with Owen?

'What will happen to you?' he had asked, and Nan shrugged.

'I have no idea, but I am not afraid, whatever my fate shall be.' She smiled. 'I have always loved my mistress and, like cousin Ina, I would willingly die for her.'

It was a gallant speech in one so young. They had all made a silent prayer that would not be the case and that Marie would keep her promise and send both women once she was safe in Northumberland as Owen's wife.

'I will never forget Lady Marie, whatever befalls.' This was all the girl had to remember when her courage and loyalty would be put to the test.

Tam was glad to see Zor as part of the crew. Leaving the great creature would have been heart-wrenching for Linmer and Marie, but William had said he could be accommodated. He had once had a small terrier, and no one objected to the captain having a pet aboard. Indeed, the crew were devoted to his little dog, petted and spoilt by strong men who would have killed humans where necessary. All this tiny creature just had to wag its tail and they were lost for ever.

But what of Mags? Tam heard a cawing and there she was far above his head, on the foremast.

At the wheel William laughed. 'Mags too. She will have her uses in the crow's nest. With her eyesight keener than any human's, she will alert us to any coming danger.'

Tam's other memory was Halcro parting with Baubie. It was such a tender moment. The tall, strong, still handsome fisherman and the ugliest woman Tam had ever seen, And yet? He remembered how she had taken care of him in his disastrous arrival at the broch, her cave that looked so dark and forbidding from the outside but was full of light inside, despite the lack of any obvious windows. And he recalled that dream when he lay sick and the beautiful young woman who looked after him so tenderly. His dream had been extraordinarily vivid and, where Baubie was concerned, one could only expect magic at work.

In the benign overture of a dying day, the ship swaying gently in the arms of a calm sea, it seemed to Tam as though she was taking the chance of closing her eyes in a quiet sleep, her breath the whispered creaks and occasional shiver of the tall timbers.

At the wheel Captain Morham was considering the map, smiling, for what interested him most in the coming adventure was far from earthly treasure but that moment when the *Falcon* would sight the Scottish coast and the cliffs of Aberdeenshire. He thought of Susannah in her castle at the Mearns and had already worked out that the creek downhill from the castle shielded by high cliffs might also be the entrance to a cave used by smugglers, a secret passage emerging in the castle courtyard and a useful way to transport their goods. He sighed happily, an excellent place to land and spend a few hours with Susannah in the comfort of her recent inheritance.

He told Tam of his plan. Tam spent a lot of time at the wheel with him, since he was curious about this new experience and had little he could do that was any use on the voyage. William was delighted to have his company, glad of his presence and his questions, for he had little time in his life to make deep friendships or lasting ones with men of his own age, although by all his calculations and despite outward appearances, Tam was old enough to be his father.

This friendship, alas, knowing what he did, would not be lasting and William felt saddened since he had developed a rapport with the time lord, a warmth of feeling renewed for this strange man from a future whose image had never left him since their first meeting when he was four years old. Although there had been many visitors over the years at Morham, none had left that lasting impression of this man, whose luminous eyes seemed to look right through him, eyes that demanded and would always see the truth beyond the words spoken. Although in the way of heroes he had always hoped and dreamt that they might meet again, it seemed unbelievable that such should ever happen and that Tam Eildor should be here at his side on the *Falcon*'s wheel unchanged by the passing years.

Now he knew the reason and never doubted Tam's story. Although what he had been told about a world that would exist some eight centuries in the future was unimaginable, his instinct told him that it was true, and though some kind of magic must be involved, he believed Tam Eildor was an honest man who he could trust.

Now, in the most important decision of his life awaiting in the Mearns, he would take Tam to meet Susannah. He would also take Marie, certain that his beloved would be impressed by marrying this man whose half-sister was a royal princess.

At his ship's wheel, captain once more, William was happy and content, certain that he could convince Susannah that this was the final voyage of the *Falcon*. With privateering past for ever, he would be returning to claim her as his bride and the new role of master of her vast estate.

Aware that he had not thought it through completely, his life and freedom as a pirate being restricted to clear thinking and planning at sea rather than any future on dry land, he vowed not to become confused or unnerved by complications that might never happen on this voyage. After loving him over several long years and waiting most patiently, he told himself Susannah would be happy and proud to be his wife, impressed that his last mission had been at His Majesty's command and the possible material benefits that this might bring to their future life.

As for Owen, he was content to be on the *Falcon* with Marie and the seas calm, under a cloudless, lazy sky on a warm day. He had only one goal. He did not care a jot about whether or not there was treasure at Fast Castle, as he saw it only as a stopping off place to travel overland to Alnwick Castle where he and Marie would be wed and made welcome by the Percys, his late mother's family. Sometimes in idle moments, he closed his eyes and pictured the magnificent wedding in the castle chapel, his slight lameness overlooked by all the Northumbrian nobility, guests at the feast afterwards. Meanwhile, he was happy to walk the decks of the *Falcon*, ready to offer help whenever needed, relieved to have seen the end of the privations of his father's rule over Orkney and his lifetime of abuse from his brothers' ridicule and scorn.

Marie approached with a smile and took her hand. She was constantly at his side. She had grown used to her boys' clothes and becoming a woman again on a sea voyage had little appeal, since breeches and a shirt were so very comfortable instead of full skirted gowns, which were less adapted to swaying walking decks and climbing ships' ladders. She regretted losing the exciting role of cabin boy but, thanks to

Owen, she also had one clear goal: to escape for ever the confinement of twelve years in the broch as her Uncle Robert's ward-cum-prisoner, with nothing to look forward to but the horrendous, unthinkable and imminent future of marriage to Patrick.

Suppressing a shudder, she closed her eyes and, leaning closer to Owen, she dreamt. Of all the treasure-seekers aboard, she had most to gain: to be Owen's wife for the rest of her life. Freedom at last! And she could enjoy a pleasant voyage out at sea, whose waves she had listened to at the broch, like a heart beating on the shore. Waves so wistfully contemplated over the years. Waves that, her prayers answered, were now carrying her swiftly far beyond Uncle Robert's cruelty.

They turned to greet Halcro. The fisherman was widely respected and looking forward to a brief return to the seas beyond Orkney. Now as pilot and boson he was the most practical and experienced as well as the most well acquainted with quayside taverns in Kirkwall, the haunt of labouring men from the shipbuilding and also the haunt of seamen looking for likely ships. He had an instinct for spotting an honest strong seaman who, like himself, had sailed before the mast. He knew the kind to avoid, too young and too idle, ready to spend their days over a free drink of ale, but not strong enough for the rigours of setting sail.

For him, the treasure business was a mere challenge; money did not greatly interest him, beyond having enough for the simple rules of his life: food and drink, the welfare of his boat and good weather for the fishing. His negotiations with Captain Morham had been successful and in his new role he intended to complete the *Falcon*'s mission to the best of his ability. Without any knowledge of the captain's plan, he had thought no further than taking ship back to Baubie, perhaps with Dr Linmer, who he imagined had reason to resume life at the broch.

Halcro's intention was, in fact, far from the doctor's. Linmer had discussed his plan for the future simply because he had an odd feeling that he was running out of time. His memory regarding past events had faded, he knew only that he had been many years stranded at the broch and it was only the advent of Tam Eildor's extraordinary arrival that touched a faint chord. How long ago or by what folly had brought him as a young man to be abandoned on Orkney, he had no idea..

He sighed deeply these days. He felt how he looked: an old man certainly, maybe already more than a hundred years in age, although he had not shown physical symptoms until Lady Marie arrived twelve years ago and he realised years were passing as he watched her emerge from child into woman.

His mind had not undergone any change through time's passing, whatever he had been in that world of the future he had lost was connected with scientific achievement too. Although in this world of the sixteenth century, it was known as alchemy and dangerously regarded by the ignorant as witchcraft, for which the unlucky perpetrators were taken and burned.

He had sent his instruments, his globes and formulae ahead on a Leith-bound ship to await his arrival. For

Leith was his destination, where he intended leaving the *Falcon* and heading the short distance into Edinburgh.

'Edinburgh!' The word was magic. A perfect goal for him to find some place and settle down for as long as his life remained.

Fortunately for the voyagers, as they set sail outward bound on their voyage, their true motives were known only to themselves, far from the treasure-seeking command of King James to the Earl of Orkney, settled once more in the gloom of Kirkwall Castle, his plans for the new Bishop's Palace once again taking prominence on his table.

The Earl was interrupted when another sudden vision of Tam Eildor forced itself up at him among his papers, arousing again those fearful doubts. Maybe he should not have let him leave but executed him on the spot. Though he thought that was not the answer.

He had been mortally afraid of the far-reaching consequences, and he now knew the reason, certain that he would be cursed in a dying man's last moment before the axe fell.

He stared into space, hoping that once the treasure was found, Owen would remember his advice and kill Tam off, tip him overboard. Meanwhile, the Earl could only look forward to the distant prospect of the ship returning with news of the treasure and concentrate on what royal gifts that future would bring.

CHAPTER NINETEEN

This was Tam's first time aboard a ship or crossing a mighty sea. Although aware of oceans on the abandoned Planet Earth, this was not only a new experience but he was soon to discover that the *Falcon* was a world of its own, with its own rules and at the mercy of the wild seas beyond Orkney.

There was a final lurch, before the sails dipped and the vessel shuddered. William called out orders to the crew as, hands on the wheel, he steered the mass of timber and sails to meet the ocean while Tam stood at the prow looking down on the fast-moving sea. He was trying to feel brave, but courage was far from his mind and he realised the inadequacy of that panic button. It would be useless now that his feet had left dry land, or in particular the Orkney beach where he landed.

Leaning on the rail, he looked down on the sea so calm and blue, it looked as if it had never heard of storm or tempest.

The weather promised to be calm, or so they all believed. There was no hint of storm or tempest so far, and with none really caring about King James's treasure, was this voyage a prelude to their dreams, or was there a vastly different future awaiting that none of them had imagined?

Halcro approached and, seeing Tam smiling, said, 'You had better become acquainted with us. The *Falcon* has a difference language at sea and you need to know the terms in daily use,' he added.

Tam followed him eagerly across decks that were daily holy-stoned, a process that made them smoother and cleaner than those in many a stately home or castle. Halcro helped make sense of many shipboard terms, clear to every seaman and regularly used in each conversation, but all of which were a foreign language to Tam, such as the nature of the leeway, the loss of windward distance in wearing and, leaning over the rail, the importance of the hawser in relation to the anchor.

Halcro went on to explain the impossibility of tacking in a very great wind and the inevitability of a leeward drift in case of being embayed with a full gale blowing. He stopped and looked sternly at Tam, who nodded and smiled weakly, completely baffled and failing to understand the horrors this situation implied.

There was little movement in the ship, beyond a slight roll and creak of the timbers as the gentle waves fell against its sides. As they walked the length from bow to stern Halcro pointed out the weather deck and the quarter deck or aft, its raised portion and, above it, the gun deck. Now empty, Tam decided it had probably seen much action in their captain's former privateering days. As if reading his thoughts, Halcro said, 'It is to be hoped we will not need that on our voyage, but it is always a good deterrent to those with piracy in mind.'

There was the forecastle and the three masts fluttering above their heads to be identified. The belaying pin, carved wooden rods set in rails as points to secure lines, the capstan, the vertical winch to haul heavy loads like the anchor and at the stern, the chip log, a wooden log trailed off the stern to measure speed.

Tam was about to interrupt with an important question about the logistics of sleep, when Halcro touched his forelock and headed towards the wheel as William approached with Owen and Marie, Zor at her side.

William indicated that they were going down below to the great cabin, the captain's quarters, and Tam should join them. He did so, amazed at how readily the huge wolf-dog had adapted to this new life, with no problems in movement and keeping balance to the ship's swaying, possibly having the advantage of moving on four legs instead of two.

Once inside the great cabin, before closing the door, William answered the question that had been troubling Tam by pointing down the narrow corridor. 'These are the crew's quarters.'

Marie gave that a moment's thought, looked at him and frowned. He laughed and took her hand. 'And this is yours, sister.'

Marie looked round, smiling. 'It is lovely, William.' And so it was: large, opulent and panelled, with poster bed, desk, table and padded armchair, all with a great window overlooking the sea.

She shook her head and said firmly, 'But I am depriving you, you are captain—'

'And it will not inconvenience me. See,' he opened the door into a smaller room more simply furnished with two small beds, 'that is extra accommodation where my cabin boy would sleep and it will do splendidly.'

He smiled, while Marie still frowned as she considered the new arrangement. Then she shook her head firmly and he saw in the set of her face determination to refuse this gallant offer.

Before she could put it into words and start an argument, he said sternly, 'I will not accept no for your answer. Do not forget who you are, Marie. Remember you are a royal princess and must expect be treated as such.' He took her hand and kissed it gently. 'As well as being my dear sister,' he added with a grin.

There was a looking-glass on the wall and it reflected them for a moment. They both regarded it solemnly and Marie sighed sadly.

'We had the same father.'

He echoed that sigh. 'Indeed, we did, and little good it did either of us.'

Marie looked again at William, a head taller than herself, strong and handsome, and her gaze returned again to their reflections. The only thing they both had inherited from Lord Bothwell, was the fine head of russet-coloured hair. Paired with William's classical fine features, inherited from his mother, the aristocratic Norwegian, Marie laughed. 'Put on a horned helmet and you would be a Viking pirate to the life.'

'I have long since abandoned that role,' he bowed and replied stiffly.

Marie giggled at her idea and then became solemn. 'We have another sadder bond than our father. Neither of us knew our mothers.'

He exchanged a sigh with Marie, who asked, 'What of Owen?'

'He is welcome to share your bed, Marie.' William laughed. 'It is big enough for two and he is your betrothed husband.'

'No, no,' said Marie sternly. 'That will not do at all. Owen has resolved that must never happen until we are wed. Even if we are to live in close confinement on this ship and yearn for each other, he will never bed me until the ring is put on my finger and in Alnwick, before his family, we are legally married, declared man and wife.'

A bell sounded on deck, and there was a different song in the gentle creaks of the ship. 'We are well under way now. Soon we will be sighting our first landfall, the northern Scottish coast. I must go.' William kissed her gently. 'Enjoy your new home, dear sister.'

'That I will do,' she whispered. As he left, she felt suddenly alone listening to the hiss of the water as the ship changed course, the slight rocking movement of the cabin's timbered walls. 'That I will do,' she echoed to no one in particular and, because she thought a prayer was in order, she closed her eyes and said, 'Thank you, dear God, for rescuing me. This is a great improvement, on what I left behind in the broch.'

She had just settled down to sleep when, from the deck above, loud noises, swift movements.

And a woman's scream.

CHAPTER TWENTY

What had happened? Running up on deck, with Zor at her side, Marie saw that it was not as bad as what she feared. She had carried a nightmare that had stayed with her since she joined the *Falcon*, worried that Uncle Robert had found out that she had escaped, had intercepted the ship and was carrying her back to the broch. This became even worse when she imagined being married to Patrick, abandoned to his tender mercies at Kirkwall Castle.

As she emerged on deck, determined at all costs not to be a prisoner again, even if it involved leaping over the rail to her death, she looked around.

Where was Owen? Suddenly he appeared saying, 'Don't be afraid. We have a stowaway. A girl, just discovered. She was hiding in the rowing boat.'

Marie went with him to where the girl was standing, trying to protect her nakedness.

Like Marie she had been dressed in boys' clothes, but these were being stripped from her and she was protesting, trying to fight the men off with her fists, half naked in a man's shirt, her breeches torn away by the seamen who found her, eager and already fighting among themselves to be first to sample her charms.

William appeared. He called them sternly to order and the stowaway pushed forward now stood shivering before him.

'Take her down to my cabin, if you please,' he ordered Halcro, ignoring the angry and disappointed murmurs of the crew deprived of their spoils. It seemed the captain was to have her first, but that was his privilege and who were they to argue?

Following Halcro and the girl, with an apologetic glance in Marie's direction, William whispered, 'This won't take long. We will sort it out.'

'Let me come too,' Marie said, following them down the gangway with no idea what that sorting out could imply. Obviously, they were too far out now to return the girl to where she must have boarded the ship while it stood in readiness to sail at Kirkwall harbour.

William seated the girl in the armchair, put a blanket around her and, after a drink of the mild ale the ship carried, she started to tell her story. She was shivering, terribly afraid after having glimpsed Owen and identified him as one of Earl Stewart's sons. He had remained in his distinctive uniform on the ship for its air of authority over the crew.

Was this captain, her saviour of the moment, just another man of the same kind as the sailors who had discovered her?

There was another man there, standing by the window, a tall, imposing figure, arms folded, who was not like any of the other men. There was something about him that set his silent observation apart.

It was Marie who had taken the confusion in hand and, seeing how the girl trembled, afraid and tearful, took her hands gently. With an appealing look in William's direction, she said reassuringly, 'Don't be afraid, we will look after you.'

'What is your name?' William asked. Observing that her complexion was somewhat foreign compared to the pale Orcadians, he paused and smiled. 'I presume you speak our language.'

She nodded and smiled. 'You can call me Juna, sir captain.'

Relieved, William leant forward and said, 'And what brought you onto our ship, Juna? What is your story?'

Juna's voice was hardly above a whisper as she told them that she came from Tankerness House and had been seamstress to Lady Cora Bruce, who had died recently. The lady had taught her how to read and write.

The listeners' eyes widened that Juna had something to be grateful for, although Lady Cora's motive was doubtless for own ends, such as carrying messages and so forth.

Juna had heard about the frigate from the other

servants, being readied to sail from the harbour. She walked down to have a look and made an immediate decision, convinced that this was her only chance to leave Orkney. She had to escape as soon as possible since Patrick, the Earl's eldest son, was pestering her. And the listeners did not need to be told why.

She paused, a sudden scared look in Owen's direction. He gave her a humble bow and she saw none of the lust in his smiling eyes that she had seen in Patrick's. He had a gentle face and under the fair, unruly butter-coloured hair, he looked young and kindly. She felt that she would be safe from him.

Marie's eyes widened at Juna's piece of information that Patrick must have seen her at Tankerness House where he was searching for information about any relatives Lady Cora might have had.

When Juna paused, embarrassed, Marie had guessed the rest, that he been fascinated as was his usual way by any pretty face. But as hers was not only pretty but unusual, his intent was certainly amorous and also entirely dishonourable.

Juna's new listeners were also intrigued by her background, which she owed to a Spanish sailor who had once voyaged to the Americas with Christopher Columbus.

It was Tam who got the full story from her later. There was something about those strange eyes of his that inspired her trust and confidence, or was it because, like herself, she suspected that he belonged to another world?

187

Once with a ship of his own, the cruel man who was her father had returned to the south of the New World believing there was gold in plenty to be stolen. He had taken her and her mother, the daughter of a native chieftain, and brought them back as slaves. The ship was wrecked on Orkney and all were lost but herself and her mother, who swam like all their tribe in the lake of their homeland. However, because of their darker complexions they were dismissed as savages and they were forced into service, working in the kitchens of Tankerness House.

Since her mother died two years ago, Juna's dream was to make her way somehow back to her tribe in the New World. How she was to accomplish this was beyond her means or indeed only the product of wildest imagination.

When Patrick had encountered her, she recognised the lust in his eye. His attempts to touch her wereh she stubbornly evaded. Tam could understand her appeal to any male eye. She was a beautiful girl, her appearance considerably more alluring, he guessed, than Patrick's pale-skinned mistress and undoubtedly that of his late wife.

Patrick had been determined to have her and by now she was well aware of the dangers that rejection of any advances made by the Stewart sons could have. Servants had no rights and were treated by the Earl as merely pieces of property. She guessed the dire consequences in store for any girls who refused their advances.

Once she saw the ship she decided she would take this last chance of escape. Perhaps it was what the Great

Spirit had willed, that stowing away on the *Falcon* would be her first step into returning to her beloved homeland.

'How did she imagine she ever could do this, get to the other side of the world?' William asked Tam. Both men suppressed sighs, as did the others on hearing Juna's story. Heads were solemnly shaken.

Their own quest of finding Scottish treasure was nothing by comparison with such a wild ambition. However, when questioned she said she had looked at the map on the cabin wall and believed that once in Edinburgh, the great capital of Scotland, there would be ships leaving for the New World.

Misinterpreting their frowns, she pleaded to William, 'You will not send me back, sir captain?' The captain was handsome and he had a kind face, not at all like that of the evil Patrick or the rough seamen who had dragged her out of hiding.

He said, 'Never fear, miss. Sending you back is not our intention. You must stay with us until we strike land and then we will decide what to do next in your best interests.'

'A ship for the place they call the New World, please, sir captain!' she pleaded. The stowaway's request made William smile. But even if there were such a ship, she was penniless. Could they raise enough money even amongst themselves to pay for her dream? The cost of a voyage across the Atlantic was high indeed, well beyond the means of most ordinary folk and he knew from experience that unscrupulous ship-owners and captains made fortunes from eager passengers.

He looked at Juna reassuringly and said, 'Meanwhile we must find you a place on shipboard with us—'

Marie interrupted. 'She can share the cabin with me, William.'

Juna turned to her quickly. 'No, madam.'

Marie smiled and explained the practice of trusted servants sleeping at the base of their masters' – or in this case, mistresses' – beds.

As she was speaking William nodded and signalled his satisfaction to her. Then with a frown, he regarded Juna's bare feet and legs and saw her clutch a ship's blanket closer around herself

'We should find you some clothes,' he suggested.

He cast a questioning look towards Marie, wondering how many gowns she had brought with her. Marie knew she had brought only two gowns and was wearing one of them. But she decided that even if she could spare one, fashioned for her slim, boyish figure thanks to those years of semi-starvation at the broch, it would never fit this full-bosomed girl. She said as much to William.

William stroked his chin for a moment, then beamed at the girl. 'Can you sew?' He pointed. 'There is a chest in the hold full of silks and such goods I brought—' He stopped as he remembered it was amongst spoils from one of his privateering trips. 'Perhaps you could . . . ?'

'I am a seamstress, sir captain,' Juna said. 'I can make a gown for milady.'

'Not for me, for yourself,' said Marie. 'I can help you. I love to sew.' She added wistfully, 'It was one of my mother's gifts I inherited,'

William stood up, bowed and prepared to take his leave, saying to Juna, 'Lady Marie will tell you all you need to know about the ship.'

He was followed by Tam and Owen, who grinned and said, 'Well, that should keep Marie from getting bored on the voyage.'

Owen himself was never bored. The voyage was an exciting new experience since he had never been away from Orkney in his life. His five brothers had shown little desire to travel away from the dubious comfort of Kirkwall Castle on more than limited short travel between the islands.

As he and Marie seemed to spend every available moment in each other's company, even while she sewed with Juna, emerging from a sumptuous masse of bright materials, Owen happily watched over them both, threading needles and helping the two girls with scissors and threads.

He had declined sharing the small cabin next door with William and tactfully offered by Tam, who considered that having declined her bed, Owen might like to remain close by. He would hear none of it and insisted on the less elegant sleeping quarters with Halcro and Linmer, leaving Tam to share with William, an arrangement which suited the two friends admirably. With respect shared, they were always ready to share a drink together as they retired, William ever eager to hear more about that strange future world Tam had left to travel back in time and to confide in him more regarding the plan for his future once the time of meeting Susannah grew daily closer.

When Tam had asked him when he had last heard from her, he said his only communication over the past two years had been a message carried by an Aberdeen-bound merchant vessel he had encountered.

Ordinarily, Tam closed his eyes, his sleep like an extinguished candle. After wishing him goodnight, William, in the adjoining bed, would listen to his gentle snoring with some envy. Used over many years to the short periods of sound sleep the watch demanded, William always listened for the ship's bell declaring eleven o' the night and, aware of Halcro's watch at the wheel, he settled down, closed his eyes, aware that his ship was making a comfortable five knots.

Orkney had vanished, leaving the *Falcon* to sail through a series of small islands separating them from the north coast of Scotland. William's passengers found this of considerable interest when they awakened that morning, with the sea leaping in white sheets over dangerous-looking rocks and sea stacks.

Once carefully negotiated, the *Falcon* made her way into the widespread waters of the ocean where seabirds no longer followed in a sky clear of only a few moving clouds, alternating with grey mists.

It was a moment of revelation for Tam knowing that they were a tiny vessel in a world of endless water between the horizons, silent, strange and vaguely threatening. Despite the fact that it remained calm, he was conscious that they were moving across an unknown territory. Beneath them was an underwater world inhabited by a different species in this lost planet that so fascinated him.

His friends were equally interested but for them, William realised, the voyage of the *Falcon* thus far had been more like a cruise ship in the Mediterranean waters of his piracy days than touching the notorious crossing from the Orkney islands to the Scottish north-east coast.

Indeed, each time he went down to what had been his cabin and was now Marie's temporary home, he found that the great round table defied any evidence that his ship had ever been a pirate frigate and held fast the illusion of a cruising vessel for the privileged few who could afford such luxury. This was most often sons of the nobility who were sent abroad for a little worldly but costly experience before settling down to a title to inherit, a vast estate to manage and, in many cases, a dynastic marriage arranged in their childhood and based on property rather than love.

Owen had abandoned the Stewart livery and, thanks to William's well-plenished wardrobe, both he and Halcro had taken what was almost another uniform perhaps with an air of authority, sustainable and protective in all weathers; a leather jerkin, breeches and thigh boots. Linmer, however, declined William's offer and continued to distinguish the assembly by his scholar's robe and velvet bonnet.

As for the crew, they wore sheepskin suitable for sudden changes in the elements. When the weather was mild they threw these off as too warm for heavy exertions such as mast climbing, preferring to work naked to the waist.

William approved of his crew, seeing them obeying orders at the double and greeting him with respectful manner suggesting that they would give no trouble, after the incident with the stowaway. Every captain's horror was of mutiny, but here there were no rebellious murmurs that might intensify into something more dangerous, and he told Halcro that he was well pleased with the kind of men that he had chosen.

Halcro smiled and told him that it was no mere chance. From his own years at sea, he had acquired an instinct for the characters of men he had sailed with and the half-dozen met in the taverns and quayside at Kirkwall he knew to be reliable and honest, except where stowaway girls were concerned. To William he repeated how when approached all seemed eager to seize the opportunity to take ship again and leave Orkney. None expressed any great desire to know when and if the *Falcon* would return.

Tam found the crew friendly and helpful. They did not seem to regard him as different in any way from other men, although he was the only one to remain uninfluenced by the uniform changes and continued to appear in the same white shirt and leather breeches in which he had first appeared at the ebb tide on the broch, clothes. Much to Linmer's astonishment these never needed laundering, being made of some indestructible material from the future world from which Tam had travelled.

Although both shared a role of time lord Tam still surprised the old man, but at least now he had accepted Tam Eildor and no longer worried or considering him an ill-willed sinister being, merely a product of the science from the world of a new planet.

The usual scene in the cabin was a very pleasant one in those early days of sailing as they moved smoothly across a vast ocean between the horizons, and when they were alerted by one of the lookout crew pointing out a rare appearance of some large fish or mammal, Tam said this was a sure indication of an underwater sea world in the lost Planet Earth.

To the soothing music of a still gentle sea, the *Falcon*'s passengers played cards in the great cabin. Linmer was something of an expert, the others declared to Tam, who was a constant loser and saw little point in such a game. Owen, however, had bitter experience with cards, having also been humiliated as a loser when playing with his five brothers who constantly cheated.

Marie soon gave up and returned to Juna, who preferred devoting her energies to the physical business of sewing. She was not only a clever seamstress, but seemed to know all about constructing gowns out of the mass of material of silks and velvets from the discarded chest. She had even gone so far as to find white cambric and was intending a shirt with the drawstring neck that provided a fashionable ruff for Captain Morham, she whispered to Marie, as gratitude for saving her.

Marie smiled. Sometimes she looked at Juna and heard a sigh, a light of longing, the hint of first love in her eyes.

She kept her observations to herself and never commented, although it made her sad. How could she warn Juna that it was not to be, that William's heart was already taken, faithful to the love he had not seen in years?

This easy crossing, two days of pleasant sailing in long summer days, was not to last. And only William observed that the calm sea had diminished during the past hours of daylight. They lay with little movement until the morning watch, when a series of small eruptions in the smooth ocean and cold rain came sweeping from the west, bringing a moderate swell to make the *Falcon* pitch as William observed with his sea instruments that she stood now considerably to the north as well as east.

This was not by any means a new chapter in his history. He smelt trouble ahead and gave the order that those not needed on deck take refuge below from the driving rain, an order that included his passengers who did not seem unduly perturbed by what this change in the weather might forfend. Heavy rain? Well, they shrugged, for anyone who had lived in Scotland, rain was an almost daily occurrence and everyone got wet sometime or another. It was inconvenient but avoidable, so they retreated back to the cabin and the cards were reshuffled, the sewing resumed.

All that day they sailed and all day Tam, who had discovered a sensitivity to atmospherics, watched the glass in William's cabin as it dropped. When William came down off his watch, he looked solemn.

'Bad times ahead?' asked Tam.

William nodded. 'I think so, but hope not.'

He did not add that, from his pirate days, he knew what was in store where a sudden drop in temperature was the inevitable prelude to full gales. He shook his head, for rarely had it dropped so fast almost within sight of the north coast of Scotland.

Although he said little, Tam followed him up on deck and heard him giving orders to Halcro in case these would be necessary. Then, still silent and withdrawn, William kept to the stern platform and Tam joined him there, watching the western sky out on the windward beam. The wind, resembling a sudden unpredictable kind of squall the northern passengers were used to, had been replaced by a pale sunlight beating through the clouds.

Tam had sudden hopes which a glance at William's face showed was not shared, although the sun shone brightly and the *Falcon* now heeled pleasantly on the fine blue swell under a rainfall that had become a fine mist.

Sunshine was tempting and the *Falcon*'s passengers emerged from below. Tam observed Owen and Marie arm in arm oblivious of any dangerous change in the weather, walking the deck together, while William from time to time looked at the masthead. He did not wish to go up there himself, for fear of raising hopes that might be dashed, but with all his force awaiting a summons, aware that he was in a high state of tension and anxiety as he had ever experienced, the happy couple's burst of laughter sent a jet of anguish through him. However he paced on and on, his hands clasped behind his back, from taffrail to the hances and back again, and as Tam observed, he showed no signs of emotion.

But when the hail from the masthead came at last, William still paced on for a while before taking his telescope to the topgallant sail. There was no storm, but instead what they were all hoping for. And there it lay.

Landfall.

CHAPTER TWENTY-ONE

This sighting had occurred several times since leaving Orkney, the passengers delighted at the prospect of seeing land in the distance after the long stretch of sea before they would reach Scotland. William explained they were still far from their destination, merely at the northern most peak of Scotland, the crossing place to Orkney. There was still two sides of a great triangle for them to round before descending towards the Aberdeenshire coast and their first destination.

He knew that the fault lay with good weather having lulled them into such happy security until the recent rainfall. There was to be an alarming change that only William and Halcro, with their long experience, both recognised beneath a sea's smiling calm the other devil's face one must be aware of.

As the swell steadily increased, so did the mildly

pleasant breeze become something stronger and William knew well that once the wind came on to blow, the clouds in the west could cover the sky with extraordinary speed and a seemingly sweet day would turn into a howling darkness full of racing water.

A quick visit to the cabin below showed him the glass lower still, sickeningly low. When he raced back on deck, he saw that he was not the only one to have noticed the mounting sea. Tam said nothing but he looked worried, his quizzical glance and raised eyebrow warning enough that he interpreted danger ahead, confirmed by an oddly disturbed sea, white water as if moved by some not very distant invisible force. The ship's bells went on all day, duly proclaiming each four hours the change of watch.

That night, the night of the new moon, a new character entered the sea stage. As they rounded the corner of the firth and on to the Scottish east coast, they were greeted by growing cloud in the west and, in the pale sky northwards, the beginnings of an aurora. With its shimmering curtain that wavered high up over the sky and faint prismatic streams perpetually falling yet always in the same place, a weird but magnificent green light was shooting from sea to sky across the horizon. Like some strange magic the sight of it in northern waters had terrified mariners of old, believing that this heralded the end of the world and that they were falling off the world's edge straight down into hell.

'Come and see the aurora,' he called and, completely mystified, the passengers seized their cloaks and trooped up on deck. There they gazed at the scene open-mouthed in wonder, as did the crew, some of whom in terror knelt down and crossed themselves, taken aback and terrified as those ancient travellers, for the flashing green lights had an unearthly yet terrifying beauty.

'What does it mean, sir captain?' Juna shivered.

William smiled down at her and said, 'Don't be afraid, it is a natural phenomenon. There is no explanation in any textbook. I have only seen it once before in all my travels on sea.'

Halcro said, 'I have seen it twice, once in summer like this off the Orkney coast while I was gathering in my nets.'

'Will it affect our voyage?' Owen asked anxiously.

'Not in the least. It will soon begin to fade.'

'Like a rainbow,' said Tam, who had only read about rainbows but never seen one. The aurora was even more impressive by its rarity and still ahead growing in streamers of unearthly splendour.

'What does it mean?' they wanted to know, weather-wise or otherwise.

William smiled. 'No one knows, but the rainbow as I recall was God's message that he would never destroy the world by flood after Noah took to the ark.'

Marie crossed herself and whispered, 'Sweet Jesus.'

William took her hand. 'Let us take this as a good omen. That we will be lucky.'

'Not lucky, brother, blessed,' she whispered.

'Very well. Let us take it as a sign that our voyage has His blessing.'

Tam found it difficult to sleep that night. From his cot-like bed, he kept his eye on the tell-tale compass William had installed overhead.

He had not been staring long before deep thunder joined a heavy rainfall, turning it into a roaring storm. He could feel the crash of the seas on the *Falcon*'s side and the song of the innumerable taut lines and ropes that communicated their general voice to her hull were resounding and took on a deeper note the rush of the larboard watch to take up their duties after four hours' sleep.

Almost at once the *Falcon* fell off to where the wind's voice almost died away, slower and slower to where it steadied and the ship was on the starboard tack, flanking across the sea with a lively corkscrew motion. There they lay with little movement until the morning watch, when cold rain came again, sweeping from the west and a moderate swell that pitched the ship gently north as well as east.

All the while the passengers remained in happy ignorance of what lay ahead, as the glass in William's cabin continued to drop in the same manner that had foretold in his pirate days. Rarely had it dropped so fast on northern waters before.

When he had taken the precautions the case would admit, Halcro at the wheel, William kept to the deck at the stern, where Tam joined him as he watched the western sky out there on the windward beam, and all the while the sun still shone brightly and the *Falcon* heeled pleasantly on the fine blue swell.

William found Tam's presence a great comfort and he constantly marvelled at the destiny that had brought his childhood hero unchanged, twenty years later to share his life. Meeting him again had seemed a miracle, the answer to a prayer that the man at his side unchanged by time had become his closest friend.

But for how long? Their original meeting was measured in a short time, but he had realised in one of their conversations that it couldn't be long before Tam's time mission was ended and he would vanish, returned to his own time. The space where he had stood, empty.

Tam realised this sadly too. He had made few friends in his previous visits to Planet Earth, certainly none with the depth of respect and admiration he shared with William and he found it strange to realise that his time in Orkney before they left for the voyage was numbered in days. He couldn't count exactly how many, but it hadn't taken long to form such a friendship. And so, it must end soon; he would return to his own time while William's lifetime would continue as he married to the love of his life.

Owen and Marie came on deck and walked from bow to stern, their heads close in deep conversation, while Tam observed how William from time to time looked up at the masthead, shaking his head like one awaiting an urgent summons.

It came at last. The north-westerly gale had built up a wicked sea and for two nights and a day the *Falcon* had been lying under a close-reefed main topsail and no more, her topgallant masts struck long since and her fore topsail on deck, her head to the north.

It came in full force that night and each time a tall wave struck her larboard bow, its white head racing towards her in the pitch-black night, solid water poured over her waist, tearing at the double lashed boats and spars and forcing her to head off to the north-north-west. But every time she came up again to within four points of the wind to labour and wallow as the water poured from her scuppers.

The coast was no great way off in the leeward darkness – black reefs, block cliffs and the huge waves breaking to an enormous height upon them. Just how far off, no one could tell, for no observation had been possible in this low racing murk. Yet they felt the loom of the land and many an anxious eye peered south.

William remembered how in the past the *Falcon* had a rough time of it in such seas on other voyages, tossed and bucketed about like a skiff, particularly in the early part of the blow, when the north weather came shrieking across the western swell, cutting up a confused, tumbling cross-sea that heaved in all directions until she groaned again..

But her trials were coming to an end, the howl of the wind in her rigging had dropped half an octave, losing the hysterical edge of malignance, and there were a few breaks in the clouds.

William had been standing in streaming wet under the stern break for twelve hours past. Tam came on deck and, with a smile, William handed him the sextant he had been holding under his arm, which he had been teaching Tam to use.

He said, 'Watch it closely. It is already set to something near the position of Aberdeenshire.'

Tam heard the jubilant note in his voice. Their destination close at hand. And in the hope of a fleeting glimpse through the rifts, the fixed star of the magnetic north appeared racing madly through a long, thin gap, just long enough for him to bring it down to the horizon.

'Look at it now, Tam.' To be sure, Tam saw that his horizon was far from perfect, more loosely resembling a mountain range than an ideal line. Even so the reading was better than William had hoped and he returned wordlessly to the wheel, the figures turning smoothly in his mind, checked and rechecked with the same satisfying result.

Moving into the glow of the binnacle light he stared into the hourglass as the last grains of sand ran out. He watched one of the men bent low against the driving rain and spray hurry forward, holding tight to a lifeline stretched fore and aft, and strike seven bells in the middle watch. It was half past three in the morning, and as the man reached for his speaking trumpet to call all hands to wear ship, William called, 'Stay! Half an hour will make no difference. Wear her at eight bells.'

With a sober, contained triumph, he gave the order for steadily packed sail after sail until the *Falcon*'s masts complained in spite of their extraordinary support. To Tam's surprise – water being a shifting ballast at the best – she was astonishingly swift and once her vast mass had gathered its momentum, the *Falcon* ploughed fast across the sea.

It was enough for her to ride at single anchor, given good holding ground and a moderate tide. Nearer and nearer still with the land on the larboard side. Before dinner the most northerly shore was visible from the deck right down to the white line where it met the sea.

William considered the situation. Did he have it well in hand? When should he reduce sail to let the boson get at the precious hawsers? Could he ask the exhausted crew to strike the topgallant masts down on the deck against the expected blow and then call upon them for unknown exertions when it came to securing the ship? How did the tides run in these uncharted waters?

The threat grew stronger in the west; lightning flickered on the far horizon, far but not so very far. The feeling of the day had changed and a mistake in the next hour might cost the ship her life, as well as all his precious human cargo of friends.

And a strange green colour in the curl of the waves and in the water slipping by. He glanced north-west and there the sun, though shining, still had a halo with sun-dogs on either side. But down below him and here on deck, he caught an atmosphere of larboard cathead plunged on the bow on the leeward swell. And now the surf was rising higher on the weather face of the headland. The howl in the rigging was louder.

Tam had managed to keep his feet on deck and observed the broad expanse of water between the *Falcon* and the distant landfall, which showed more white than green. Inshore where there had been smooth water not half an hour before, there was now the ugly appearance of a tide-rip, a long, narrow stretch of pure white that raced eastward from the headland and grew stronger, broader and fiercer as the tide reached its full flow.

The situation had changed indeed.

But worse was coming and coming very fast.

CHAPTER TWENTY-TWO

A grey haze overspread the sky with the speed of a curtain being drawn, followed by tearing cloud. The lightning increased on the starboard beam, much nearer now, and right ahead, a white squall, the forerunner of the full mighty gale, swept over the mile or two of the sea northwards, veiling the land entirely.

It was no longer a question of how or where William should negotiate the tide-race, but of whether he should be able to approach the land at all, or whether he should be obliged to put the ship before the ever-increasing wind and run before it.

Speed was everything. In five or ten minutes at this rate of increase there would be no alternative – he would either have to put before the wind or perish, and in any case the *Falcon* would almost surely founder in the kind of seas that would build up before nightfall.

The tide-race was cutting up higher still, as nasty as ever he had seen, yet the *Falcon* must go through it. Go through or run, and running would mean the end was only somewhat delayed.

William made his decision, it had formed clear cut in his mind and now he was quite calm and lucid, if somewhat detached. Speed was all and the only question was whether the sails and masts could drive the water-logged hull hard enough without giving way, whether the *Falcon* could race that mile of sea before it reached full force and either flung her on her beam ends or forced her to run due east. It was a desperate choice, if any sail above the foremast gave, if the oar should yield, or any upper mast, then all was lost. But at least the choice was made and he believed it was the right one. He only reproached himself for not having driven her faster and sooner, for having lost precious minutes earlier in the day.

With the greater speed she gave a cumbrous leap forward, like a carthorse spurred, and ploughed on faster still. The wind was now abaft the beam and she buried her bow so that the green seas swept over the forecastle. She was madly over-pressed, but so far could just bear it and was now racing through the tall waves, their white crests tearing head high across her waist. A gust on the rise laid her over so that her lee-rail vanished in the foam. William gave her another point – he could afford it – and now she tore towards the terrible zone where the gale screamed round the headland with redoubled force and joined the tide-rip.

At this point the adverse forces reached their highest pitch; the likelihood of being dismantled was very great. A quarter of a mile to go, the gale rising every second, the topgallant gave an appalling lee-lurch as it was sheeted home. There was a moment's pause, like the suspension of life before a fall, and then she hit the tide-rip and staggered as though she had struck ice. All round them was the roar of breaking water and an intolerable wind, bursting seas on either hand. Then she received a knock-down blow as the counter eddy took her full aback, in a confusion of water, green and white, spray covering her entirely and as it settled. But at last she was through, rocking in the smooth water under the lee of the high cliff.

Tam, still clinging on, looked at William and Halcro and laughed. The transition was unbelievably abrupt. At one moment the *Falcon* was among bursting seas, furious winds howling upon her, the next she was gliding along in silence beneath the shelter of an enormous cliff, her masts still swaying like inverted pendulums from the momentary counterblast that had knocked him into the scuppers.

William glanced aloft – the upper masts had held – and then leant far out over the rail to view the land. It tended westward towards a bay whose narrow mouth was almost closed by high cliffs. There was almost no other sound apart from the water lipping along the side and the cry of the sea birds, the ship still running fast on her own momentum. An island studded sea, high overhead the wrack of a full western gale with thunder in the clouds;

down here an unnatural calm as if the world was deaf.

In another mile the *Falcon* had almost lost steerageway. The sky was now almost as low as the high cliff and a thin drizzle floated down. Her masts hung limp, but from the mist of rain it was clear that a small breeze, a back-breeze, drew in with the land. They set the topgallants to take it and so she glided on. The bottom shelved steadily, always with the good shelly sand, and she approached a passage through the islands that closed the mouth of the bay, a clear, deep-water passage, a purse-like bay opening wide from its narrow mouth, a deep inlet sheltered on three sides. From the motion of the spume and the current it was plain that the tide was making still. It did not mean to run her on a shoal if care could prevent it.

There was a long pause while the *Falcon* ghosted still farther in, then William said, 'Down with the helm. Let go.' The anchor splashed down and the hawser ran out as the *Falcon* stopped, brought up with a mild jerk that nevertheless staggered the crew where they stood. The hawser rose and, straightening, took the full strain. This was the crucial moment. Would the anchor hold?

It did and the seamen breathed out a general sigh. Yet still the turning tide could swing her, wrench the anchor from its hold and fling her onto the islands close at hand.

'Make all fast,' came the order.

They had reached their destination.

Or so they believed, from the delighted exclamations of the passengers as they came on deck to see, but the approach of landfall was not yet as far south as they hoped. Although there was the distant prospect of vague shapes denoting spires and perhaps towers, they had merely turned the corner of northernmost Scotland and tomorrow they would be within sight of Aberdeenshire.

'A while yet to go.' William put down his telescope and, unrolling the map, pointed out that the ship was a few miles out from Fraserburgh, the most notable fishing port on the north-east tip of Scotland.

The *Falcon*'s masts swayed lazily in a gentle breeze on this mild, sunny day. A slight mist on the horizon indicated there was warmth to come and the passengers, keen to take full advantage of such excellent conditions, remained on deck.

A few hours later and a further distant sight of more populated areas declared Peterhead, the thin pencil-like shapes of masts and the hovering seabirds indicated a busy fishing fleet in its harbour.

The sight of such activity aroused the passengers' eagerness into a restless desire to step onto dry land again, to set firm footholds on the shore.

They were rewarded, as the Aberdeenshire coast offered a short sanctuary. William's telescope revealed a shining beacon, to warn vessels of the dangers of a rock-strewn, sea-stacked approach, but also to indicate that this was the tiny harbour at Slains.

William greeted the sight of that beacon with joy and he ordered a signal gunshot to announce their arrival. The laird of Slains Castle was a friend of his piracy days and many less easy encounters with this north-east coast.

* * *

From a vantage point, Francis Hay had heard their arrival and, through his telescope high in the castle, he identified the *Falcon*, this time flying not the black flag but the respectable Scottish ensign.

At the return signal to approach the passengers were informed by William that they were to prepare to make landing. He steered carefully and negotiated the entrance to the tiny harbour, a sudden lurch signalling they had arrived.

The small boat was launched and the passengers scrambled down the rope ladder. They were helped aboard by William, who would row them across, with Tam at the second oar, a novel experience he was unlikely to have again. Zor decided to swim ashore.

Halcro had elected to stay with the crew as well as Juna, who delicately declined the invitation to join those in the small boat. She had urgent sewing on hand, to finish the shirt she was secretly making for William. She had eyed the cabin's great table suddenly to be empty, as a great opportunity not to be missed, perfect to spread out materials for a gown and a petticoat for Marie.

With William and Tam as rowers, finding a strong post to firmly fix the boat for their return, Marie, Owen and Linmer reached the sandy shore and, carrying their boots, scrambled through the shallow water on to dry land, having a short spell of walking unsteadily as they got back the use of their land legs. With four legs Zor had no such problems and celebrated this return to land and the prospect of proper exercise by racing along the sandy beach.

Mags, too, was again in evidence. Having watched them land from the *Falcon*, she now flew alongside, a happy magpie at last, after a long sojourn in Marie's cabin. She had been placed inside a cage to be safe during the storm, away from her chosen spot on the highest mast, her usual perch on calm days where she sat ruffling her feathers like a disapproving dowager.

On the beach, Owen swept Marie off her feet, laughing delightedly, and the pair helped Linmer who, clutching his staff in one hand, was trying to keep his long robe out of the water.

As they donned their shoes again, they were in shadow, the castle invisible at the top of a steep cliff. They looked at William and, knowing what they were thinking, he shook his head.

'It's a stiff climb, but there is no other way. However, it will be worth it. Francis will have food and wine waiting to welcome us,' he added reassuringly.

And so, they set off, Owen and Marie in the lead, moving swiftly ahead, and even Linmer could not resist the invitation, assisted by Tam and William, with only several stops to gather breath. Zor climbed effortlessly well ahead and Mags was already cawing encouragingly from the cliff top.

At last, they clambered across the peak and, pausing breathlessly, thankfully observed the castle. Tam was again amazed at Marie's resilience and physical strength during that climb and the way she had endured the voyage and the storm, strength doubtless from her tough Borders heritage.

She was laughing. 'So it was not built to stand the way it looked, balanced precariously on the edge of the cliff after all.'

'Merely an illusion to keep invaders or pirates at bay,' said William, leading the way to where it stood a hundred yards further ahead. As it drew nearer Tam realised that, as castles went, it was several centuries old and the condition of the exterior walls suggested a constant battle with the elements that had not been successfully won.

Their tired legs started to mend and their energy renew as they closed the distance to the heavy door. It opened to reveal a smiling figure shouting a greeting.

William went forward and the two men embraced. Turning, he introduced Francis Hay, omitting his title the ninth Earl of Erroll, to his elite passengers.

As William had expected, Francis was enchanted to meet Lady Marie Hepburn. Sad and disappointed at Queen Mary's brief, tragic reign, he was both impressed and honoured to bow deeply and kiss the hand of her daughter, of whose existence he had been, like most, unaware. Now, looking down into those Stuart eyes, he saw again the shadows of her tragic parents, the woman he had idolised and the man who had been his hero. He smiled sadly.

'Welcome to Slains, Princess Marie.'

'Not princess, sir, just Marie.' She was much shorter than the queen and her russet curls brought memories of her father, who Francis had met briefly after the bitter end to the Battle of Carberry Hill and Mary's abdication. Lord Bothwell, pursued by enemies on his flight north, had taken brief refuge at Slains where Francis had given him sanctuary while trying to raise help and support from the neighbouring lairds who still remained loyal to the Queen. He had hoped they would provide money and men to aid Bothwell's bid for freedom and his determination to return with an army and restore Mary to her throne.

Francis' attempts and pleas were only moderately successful. The lairds divided politically and uneasy regarding investing in a doubtful future so, pursued by enemies again, Bothwell had fled again to Orkney where once more betrayed by those he trusted and was refused sanctuary.

'Ah, William.' Francis grasped the hand of this fine young man whose only resemblance to his father was the fox-red hair.

Francis had only discovered by chance that Captain Morham was William Hepburn, the son of Lord Bothwell, while giving hospitality to the pirate captain, who had smuggled to Slains a vast quantity of excellent brandy and wines.

Francis shook his head sadly, to have known such tragedy and ended up as a pirate. He was relieved to see, as indicated by the Scottish ensign flying so proudly on that ship anchored offshore and the presence of Owen, a son of the powerful Earl of Orkney and obviously the princess's lover, that Captain Morham had endorsed a less criminal way of life.

Francis turned his attention to William's other two

passengers: an old, wise-looking man with a long white beard and a scholar's robe, but it was the young man at his side who interested and mystified him most. He would have to wait until William could answer that question as he led them towards the great hall. It was almost the only remaining part of the fast-crumbling castle which, he suspected, if drastic measures were not taken soon, would in a few years be an uninhabitable ruin.

The visitors were introduced to two young boys who were to share their meal and it was then that William was again aware of the empty chair and the absence of Anne, Francis' wife, lost in childbirth with her daughter, who had died with her.

Francis' attention was suddenly drawn to the big dog Zor, always close to Marie's side, whose presence had aroused a chaos of shrill barking from his own two dogs. Calling on them to be silent, he patted Zor's head.

'A fine animal you have there. Oh no, allow him to remain,' he added as his own two hounds trooped after them, ignored by Zor. Tam noticed after the initial clamour had died down, they kept a safe distance from him at Marie's side, and took up their positions lying down nearby, in hopeful nearness of any food that might descend from the table.

Tam saw that Mags was not in evidence, having declined to follow her beloved Marie inside the castle. Somewhat suspicious of interiors she was sitting well away from the humans, waiting patiently on one of the corbels outside, and Tam fancied there might be something in her reactions which touched on his own.

One footstep inside the castle and he had felt an oppression. There was a bad energy bearing down on him and, always sensitive to atmospheres of ancient buildings and churches, he knew that this was not a good place. Despite this friend of William's, kind, hospitable Francis, there were ominous shadows that humans could not see, presences that were alien, ghosts they might be called, thankfully not visible or felt by their genial host. Now, Tam remembered from his addiction to ancient literature from Planet Earth that Slains Castle had a bad reputation and that the author Bram Stoker, who stayed in its successive rebuilt version some centuries later, had made its reputation worse by using it as the inspiration for *Dracula*, his vampire novel.

Tam was directed to a seat opposite the laird at the great table, its surface now scratched and scarred, was centuries old and had once been part of the original castle. The servants had prepared a repast at short notice for the visitors. There was wine not ale, with fresh meat, bread, cheese, and to the guests this seemed a feast indeed after their waning provisions on the ship. As they thanked him profusely, he said to William, 'I have ordered what are leftovers, if any remain, to return to the ship with you.' He laughed as he looked down the table, aware of the speed at which these distinguished and hungry voyagers were eating second helpings.

William thanked him and finished explaining in as few words as possible the reason for this voyage at the King's command, to discover the whereabouts of the

King Philip of Spain's treasure ship that vanished so mysteriously on its way to the Scottish capital.

Francis laughed. 'I wish you joy of that. It has been rumoured for years and I think it will remain a rumour only.' Then, indicating Tam, he said, 'And how does that young man fit into your plan?'

Remembering his promise to keep secret the time lord's identity, William replied, 'He was shipwrecked on Orkney, a vessel that got caught in a storm and went down in Kirkwall, near the broch where Marie was living.' He spared Francis the details of her confinement over the years and continued, 'The Earl is her uncle, the Queen's half-brother. The former King James was father to them both.'

'And numerous others, by all accounts. He certainly spread the Stewart dynasty,' Francis said with a smile. He gazed down the table. 'So, Owen is a cousin, too, and you and Marie have the same father.' He frowned. 'All a bit complicated, these close relationships. But they seem to be working well together.'

CHAPTER TWENTY-THREE

A distant gunshot put an end to what was a convivial meal and indicated that it would soon be time to leave. The tide was turning and with it the *Falcon* must set sail again, William told Francis.

His host sighed. 'I have few guests and would most willingly extend your stay.' He added with a frown, 'I am sure we have beds enough.' However, he was somewhat doubtful about the condition of those unused bedchambers.

Shaking hands with Tam Eildor, he would have liked to know more of this young man with such extraordinary eyes. They made him uneasy. He had never seen anyone so weirdly out of place and, indeed, out of time. Afterwards he realised what Tam Eildor reminded him of: those strange icons in ancient churches.

As they went back down the spiral staircase, at the

great door, he asked William, 'Do you remember my walled garden?'

William did, it was sheltered carefully from the shrill east winds.

Francis said, 'I have fruit ready for being harvested. Take some with you.'

That sounded like a very good idea as they were running short of provisions, and fresh fruit was a non-existent luxury until they reached a port with a marketplace.

'There is a shed across there with fruit stored, apples as well as strawberries, which grow so well in Aberdeenshire. Take as much as you need.'

At once the passengers took his advice, and the baskets he produced were packed full of fruit that would be so welcome on their return but would present an immediate problem of the steep cliff down to the shore.

Francis was prepared for that and servants were summoned to accomplish this task. As the guests exchanged anxious glances, Francis smiled and said, 'There is an easier way.' He indicated a narrow track that zigzagged steadily downwards. 'The servants are used to it. It adds a little distance but makes a considerably safer descent in bad weather.'

The crew were delighted to see the provisions unloaded from the small boat, especially after their initial disappointment, quelled by Halcro with an extra rum ration, that they were not at liberty to go ashore and explore the tiny village of Slains below the high cliff. They'd been certain of a tavern to enjoy a little refreshment and perhaps more while they awaited the captain and his guests to return.

Halcro had his own reasons for staying with the ship and they included, as he knew only too well, the dangers involved that the men, although loyal to the captain and the ship, once ashore and without a leader could be lured away, tempted to listen to rumours and strike landward to a city still some miles away, such as Aberdeen, where there would be plenty to delight them. With little inclination to return to the rigours of Orkney, the port would provide ample opportunities of taking the ship to a variety of more desirable destinations.

As the *Falcon* cast off with the outgoing tide, William's mariner instinct detected that the promise of a good spell of weather might get them as far as Aberdeen and beyond the few miles to the Mearns. He smiled at the thought; the sooner the better to be with Susannah.

Tam spent much of the day on deck leaning on the rail where he had become better acquainted with the sea on which they sailed. A strange world indeed, a sea that had swallowed many ships in its time – in fact a regular diet – and would swallow many more, but today, he thought it wore a kindly face of gentle white-tipped waves as the ship weaved a pattern through the water.

This was the kind of weather the *Falcon* could deal with, William told him, having come to his side. The north-easterly was nothing new to her, a stiffish wind that kept the sails alert. During the night the crash of the seas on the *Falcon*'s side and the song of the innumerable taut lines and ropes that communicated their general voice to her hull were resounding and took on a deeper note.

Almost at once the *Falcon* fell off to where the wind's voice almost died away, slower and slower to where the ship was on the starboard tack, flanking across the sea with a lively corkscrew motion.

William carried out his inspection with a sober, contained triumph that he was almost at an end of what would be his last voyage as commander of the *Falcon*, his last days as a ship's captain, as in the foreseeable future all of this would be part of a dangerous, colourful past that he would gladly forget.

He climbed down and gave the order for steadily packed sail after sail until the *Falcon*'s masts complained in spite of their extraordinary support. To his surprise – water being a shifting ballast at the best – she was astonishingly swift and, once her vast mass had gathered its momentum, ploughed fast across the sea.

Tam always remained on deck as much as possible, having learnt each day more and more of seamanship from William, but he was also aware that this was to be his first and last voyage. He had almost given up worrying about what the future held. He wished to look no further than each day, for the voyage which, despite the storm, he had enjoyed in the company of the people who were now his friends. William he would most regret losing and he realised once again that returning to his own time was no longer an anxiety. He was confident that Halcro would see the *Falcon* safely back to Orkney and the beach at the broch after their mission.

While they sailed, the passengers continued their daily pursuits, sitting on deck in a sheltered spot when the sun shone or, when the sky darkened for a sudden shower, retreating to the great cabin to play cards, with Marie marvelling at Juna putting on the final touches to her latest creation.

They were not far out to sea, daily riding down the coast of Aberdeenshire keeping within sight of the coast's main cities with their huddle of ships' masts crowded in harbours.

Just a few miles to go. On, on and towards William's longed-for destination, the Mearns. Even with the *Falcon*'s leeway head, no doubt this was the current setting at what he judged to be close on two miles and he could still fetch well to the windward of the land.

From his telescope, further south and east a massive cliff heaved up. The sight of a high land and black rock broad on the larboard bow convinced him, certain that this was the landfall he had prayed for since leaving Orkney.

Here his dear Susannah, like himself, awaited the end of years of patient longing at the Mearns. Although this would be a short visit, it was but a prelude to the rest of his life with her, the end of his sailing days on the *Falcon*, when as a married man he became a landowner to help his wife run the vast estate she had inherited.

He called his passengers on deck. They were in sight of it now. Heart thumping, he pointed out a tiny tower house on top of a hill, the approach by sea through a huddle of steep rocks including one William identified as the Stack, which was in fact a very large cliff. There was no place that they could take the *Falcon* in, the approach through rocks and rough seas was impossible, so it was decided that they should anchor in safe waters and William would once more give the order to let down the small boat. He would row across to the tiny harbour of the fishing village and then walk up the steep slope to the tower house.

Preparing to leave he said, 'We could have got closer; there is reputedly a cave somewhere in those rocks, used by smugglers which comes right up into the courtyard.' He had always intended to take Marie with him, certain that Susannah would be impressed by meeting the Queen Mary's daughter.

Marie, however, was not tempted by the suggestion. 'No,' she said firmly, but with a gentle smile added, 'It is not fitting, William. I will remain here with the others.'

William wondered whether it was another rowing boat approach that put her off, or the stiff walk up to the tower. Aware of his disappointment, Marie said, 'I do not think that is a good idea, William. This is a meeting that is very intimate between lovers long separated.' She smiled across at Owen, aware that he approved her decision and was nervous at letting her ashore and out of his sight.

He said, 'Marie is right. I don't think either of you would appreciate an audience, William.'

'Especially Susannah,' Marie continued. 'You go and meet your destiny, dear brother.' She stroked his cheek fondly. 'I will stay on the *Falcon* with my destiny,' she added, gazing across at Owen, now in deep conversation with Halcro regarding tide times for William's return.

As she went to join them, William bit his lip and said suddenly to Tam, 'Will you come with me?'

Tam thought it an odd request until William said, 'I need someone with me, Tam.' He paused and whispered, 'Now that this moment I have so longed for is upon me, frankly, I am scared to face it on my own.' Embarrassed, he paused and laid a hand on Tam's arm. 'And I am sure Susannah will enjoy meeting you.'

Tam failed to see the reason in that, but could understand that in a moment of great decision William needed an ally. He recalled reading that on Planet Earth, men had what they called 'stag parties' on the eve of their wedding, gathering their men friends for an orgy of drinking. Presumably this curious custom had already been established many centuries before.

William went on, 'This is the most important moment in my whole life, Tam, the moment I have dreamt of, and you are my closest friend.' He stopped and smiled. 'Please, I want to have you with me.'

The other passengers lined up at the rail. Linmer knew how much this meant to William. It was far more vital than any search for the Spanish treasure, the real reason he was making this voyage. Owen and Marie could understand William's anxiety, as lovers and close to him, his emotions echoed their own future uncertainty. Marie embraced him and, wishing him every good fortune, watched as the boat descended from the ship's side with William and Tam rowing across to the tiny harbour.

Marie took Owen's arm. 'I am glad he has Tam with him.' She was particularly anxious for, despite William's certainty that Susannah was over there waiting for him, she had grave doubts, fears that he had set so much upon this meeting and gambled his future on a message sent years ago. 'It's a long time for a woman on her own with so many responsibilities of a vast estate to wait,' she said, when their conversation drifted, as it did quite frequently to the subject of her half-brother's future.

Owen agreed. 'It is a long time for anyone, with nothing more certain than a message sent on a ship heading for Aberdeen, if it was ever delivered. Not even a person William knew and could trust, a mere stranger, eager to take his money, no doubt,' he ended gloomily.

His secret thoughts, never to be discussed with his beloved Marie, were that William was being rather too trustful based on his own experience, brought up as he had been in an atmosphere where truth was of little importance and lies in regular supply from his father to his five brothers. He knew only too well there could be many changes of heart and of circumstance.

The two rowers headed silently towards the shore, with rather too much on their minds for cheerful conversation. William was now in a state of high anxiety and Tam shared the secret misgivings of Owen and Marie.

His friend should not be setting his whole future on this meeting. He wished he could warn him, but there was no possibility or opportunity of doing so. That should have been done long ago, while it had been William's habit to turn every conversation back to Susannah. Yet when questioned he did not even remember the colour of her eyes and thought vaguely perhaps they were blue.

In truth he knew so little about her and Tam would only be released from his own fears the moment that he saw them together and knew all was well, that the happy ending William had long dreamt of was in store.

The boat safely moored, William began to look around. Had he expected Susannah to come down and meet him? Tam asked.

William laughed and said not really, but Tam realised that he had expected to see her waiting on the shore after the gunshot from the *Falcon* had announced their arrival.

As they walked up the steep road, William a little ahead, his anxiety making him almost run the last few yards, Tam's feelings of unease grew steadily as a heavy grey cloud hovered above them. They were in shadow and it felt like an omen.

As the tower house came into view, a tall, narrow building with high windows pointing seaward, Susannah was not in evidence. William gazed everywhere and gave Tam a bewildered look before knocking on the door. He said cheerfully, 'I expect she missed the signal. I will try again.'

As he did so and they waited, he stood back and looked at the frontage. 'It's very handsome, is it not? It was built in the thirteenth century. Don't you think that it stood the survival of two hundred years remarkably well?'

Tam nodded absently and thought better of his poor, anxious friend for surviving the test of two minutes.

At last, a sound of locks, a creaking and the door opened.

William rushed forward, laughing, ready to bow and embrace his love, but instead he found that he was looking into the wrinkled face of an old serving man.

'Her ladyship?' William asked. 'Did my signal shot arrive – from my ship?' he asked anxiously.

'It did indeed, sir.' The old servant bowed. 'Her ladyship is aware of your arrival. If you will please follow me,' he added and, beckoning them into the dark interior, led the way down short flight of stairs and along a long gloomy passageway constructed on a barrel-vaulted design.

'This is your first visit to the castle, sir?'

William said, 'Yes,' and the old man beamed at him. A few steps further on they passed a door on heavy iron hinges, and he pointed out what they had guessed already. 'This is our dungeon, not in use at the present moment,' he chuckled.

They moved on towards the sound of chatter and the clash of tins. A smell of cooking indicated a busy kitchen. 'As you can hear, sir, a meal is in preparation.'

Opening the door, so that they could look in, he

pointed to a very large walk-in fireplace. 'There is a concealed stairway there, leading to the upper regions so that meals can be carried directly into the great hall. A most happy convenience,' he said proudly and bowed. 'That, however, is not our destination.'

William was walking swiftly ahead and Tam was aware of his growing impatience at his unrequested tour. It was clear the tower house had few visitors and the old servant enjoyed the rare chance of showing them around.

At last, the man opened the door into a large chamber where he explained, 'This is where merchants and visitors have always waited to be seen by the laird. If you will kindly be seated—'

'Her ladyship?' William interrupted.

'Her ladyship is aware of your presence and will be with you presently,' said the old man and, with a rather offended look, he left them.

William ignored the rather hard-looking benches and paced the room back and forth.

There were light footsteps, the door opened and William rushed forward. 'Susannah—'

A young woman, another servant by her attire, bowed. 'Her ladyship is in her room at present and apologises for the delay in receiving you.'

As she curtseyed and left, Tam seized William's arm, for it seemed that he was about to rush after her.

'Wait, William—'

'I have already waited too long,' William snapped indignantly, shrugging off Tam's restraining arm. 'I am sorry, Tam,' he groaned, 'but this is not the reception I hoped for. What on earth can be delaying her?'

Tam shook his head. 'The ways of ladies preparing to meet unexpected visitors, William, we must bear with them.' Although his words were intended to be consoling and soothing, he could well understand his friend's distress, since he had imagined that Susannah shared his eagerness for this meeting.

Now, Tam's uneasiness was taking on an edge of horror. Surely William must have guessed that there was something seriously amiss, and that she should have been waiting to rush down and greet this love of her life. Instead, Tam was aware that William's love dream of a lifetime was fast turning into a nightmare.

The door opened again. William leapt to his feet, his eager smile quickly fading as another servant approached, laid wine and refreshments on the table, curtseyed and disappeared before she could be questioned.

Tam poured the wine and handed a goblet to William, who shook his head.

'No.'

'Come, William. It is excellent – far better than any we have—'

William seized the goblet, downed it in one and repoured another measure, his hand shaking. Tam regarded him anxiously, he looked close to tears.

Then, a moment later, the door opened. She had come down at last.

'Susannah, my dearest,' William cried, but Tam saw as she evaded his embrace, the expression of embarrassment and something more than that, in her startled glance.

'William, I saw you arrive. I am sorry to have kept you. Who is your friend? Aren't you going to introduce us?' This came out of her in one frantic breath and Tam, standing well aside in the shadows and hoping to remain unobtrusive, saw one thing clearly now: there was no hope left for William. It was dead, if it had ever existed.

Susannah did not and possibly never had loved him and whatever had happened had been a colossal misunderstanding and William's own fault. Tam realised the bitter, sour ending as all William's dreams plummeted to earth.

William recovered enough to bow and introduce him. 'Tam Eildor, my friend.'

Tam bowed over her hand, and saw a small, slender woman in her thirties, fair hair and blue eyes, but not one for a man's second glance. She was quite ordinary, hundreds or thousands like her in any town and certainly nowhere near the acclaimed beauty of William's dream.

Susannah remembered her manners and forced a smile. 'Do sit down. Some wine, gentlemen?' They both shook their heads and, stepping into the required role of hostess, she asked politely, 'Have you come far?'

William was too shaken still to go into details regarding the voyage of the *Falcon*.

He said, 'Susannah, I understood that we were betrothed. I came here with the intention of confirming our wedding plans. Did you not receive the message I sent you some weeks ago?'

She shook her head. 'I never received any letter or message from you, I have heard nothing since your visit all those years ago.'

A faint blush spread over her face, suggesting to Tam that it had been a very interesting meeting and that Susannah had been a great lover to convince William, a pirate at sea for long periods deprived of a woman, that this was the love he had been waiting for. So when he left, it was with the belief that she was to be his wife.

The same thought was obviously going through William's mind. He stretched out his hand attempting to touch her shoulder and she moved away rapidly.

'You said – you said—' He paused. 'You said that you loved me.'

'Did I?'

Susannah looked startled and embarrassed by this lapse of memory and, raising a delicate white hand to her mouth, giggled nervously. She glanced in Tam's direction eager for diversion before turning sternly back to William.

'Captain Morham, I cannot imagine what could possibly have given you such an idea.'

Almost wearily, William said, 'I believed you loved me and that you still do. Or I would not have made this journey.'

Susannah straightened her shoulders. 'Captain Morham, this is a misunderstanding on your part. You see—' she paused, looking towards the window as if it might give her support and took a great gulp of air. 'You see, sir. I am married.'

William shook his head in disbelief and cried, 'No!'

'Yes, indeed. Edgar – my husband – is a cousin.' She paused, listening anxiously, then continued: 'He is out hunting at the moment.'

And then came the hurried explanation. Cousin Edgar had been courting her before her father died, she had known him since childhood, was fond of him and, at last alone, she was overwhelmed. Again, that faint blush indicated to Tam the possible nature of that overwhelming.

'One day he arrived with a priest and we were married.' She paused and shook her head. 'It was quite sudden and so unexpected, I was not even sure then whether it was myself or my inheritance that interested him most,' she added candidly. She gave a laugh, which sounded a little forced, in which William detected a faint glimmer of hope. Cousin Edgar had married her against her will. She had been cheated; this cousin Edgar was not the love of her life.

He leant forward eagerly. 'Dearest Susannah, you have told me all I need to know. Do you realise you might get an annulment of this marriage, the promise of an earlier betrothal or on the grounds of consanguinity?'

Tam looked at him sharply. A poor excuse. Owen and Marie were cousins but such unions were acceptable by the church.

William's grip on her hands tightened. 'Don't you see, my dearest? Then we could be married, as we planned.'

She looked at him, then sat down, frowning vaguely. Shaking her head, she said, 'No, Captain Morham, that will not do at all. If I loved you, as you say, it was a girlhood mistake and a long time ago.' She stared over her shoulder at the window, and Tam thought perhaps she was remembering the glory of that first love. She turned back and smiled sadly at William.

'Anyway, it is too late now.' Sitting up straight, she sighed and touched her stomach. This unmistakable gesture to a roundness indicated that she was some months pregnant.

'I am with child, to be born at Christmas.'

They heard the sound of horses approaching. Susannah stared towards the window, took in a sharp breath and jumped to her feet.

'You must go. It is Edgar.' That sharp intake of breath, the way her hand fluttered to her mouth, while William continued to stare at her in shocked disbelief, told Tam that she had a jealous husband.

She turned to William. 'Please, go!'

But it was too late for retreat. Already there were footsteps on the spiral staircase and no other exit. The confrontation was unavoidable.

Tam put a restraining hand on William's arm when he leapt to his feet as the door opened.

Edgar came in and did not see them at first. He made no move towards his wife, no greeting, merely went to the sideboard and poured himself a glass of wine.

That told Tam a lot more about Susannah's husband, as he turned and saw the two men.

He put down the empty glass. 'Visitors, wife? And who have we here?'

'A friend,' she said, adding hastily and apologetically, 'From long ago.'

She struggled for a smile. 'This is William Hepburn, Lord Bothwell's son.'

If she hoped that would impress Edgar, since he had neither the looks nor the height of William Hepburn, she was mistaken. He was a plain, stout man, bald and wearing his mere thirty years badly. He made no attempt to bow or shake the visitor's hand, in an ill-concealed temper.

He turned to Tam. 'And who might you be, sir?'

Tam managed a slight bow. 'A friend—'

'Then I advise you and your friend of my wife's to leave immediately,' Edgar interrupted. To make the threat plain, his hand went to his sword.

As William seemed paralysed, Susannah's betrayal had deprived him and left him as one mortally wounded, Tam saw the danger and gently took his arm. While he urged his friend towards the door, Edgar continued, 'And if either of you set foot on my land again, I shall have you both horsewhipped.'

Susanna came to life again. 'Edgar, Sir William sent a message. He merely called as he was in the area—'

Edgar laughed, but there was no mirth in it. 'I intercepted that message, wife, and destroyed it.' As he opened the door, he said, 'Now, you two leave, before you deprive me of the joy of kicking you down the stairs.'

William made a gesture as if he had returned to life, stood steadily and, head down, seemed about to attack Edgar.

Edgar had been waiting for this moment. His hand shot out and encountered William's jaw. 'Go, before I take my sword to you. Go!'

Tam supported the now dazed William. They left watched by curious servants and made their way back down the hill to the boat. Tam untied it and helped William aboard, handed him the oar.

'Ready?' he asked. 'Can you manage?'

William merely stared at him, seized the oar Tam put into his hands and they rowed in silence towards the anchored *Falcon*, a breeze fluttering her sails in a mockery of welcome.

CHAPTER TWENTY-FOUR

A welcome was clearly in the minds of Owen and Marie, leaning eagerly over the rail, but one look at William's face and the darkening bruise, plus Tam's warning glance, told them that this love story was to have the happy ending so long anticipated by William. He clambered aboard and walked stiffly past them without a word, down to his cabin. They heard the door slam behind him.

'Oh dear,' Marie asked tearfully. 'Whatever happened?'

Tam told them in as few words as possible.

'Her husband sounds like a brute,' said Owen.

'Oh, poor William,' said Marie.

Tam went to the cabin he shared with William. The man did not move, but lay on his bed stiff as a corpse. Tam poured a glass of wine and said encouragingly, 'Take this. It will help,'

William's head turned towards him. 'It's too late, Tam. Nothing can help. I am a dying man.'

Tam knew that was true. William's heart had been torn out of him. He would be put together again and survive, but he would never be the same William. He had died in the tower house.

Tam said, 'Your chin looks sore.'

'It will heal.'

There was a knock on the door, which opened to reveal Juna. 'They told me you had been hurt, sir captain. Can I . . . ? Your face?' She moved nearer. 'I know about such things.'

Tam closed the door quietly behind him as he went back on deck.

Halcro had seen them arrive, guessed that William had been hurt and had given orders in his absence to set sail. It sounded like a bereavement and Linmer, who had heard the story from Owen and Marie, shook his head sadly.

'I feared for William. It was such a long time, and he had gambled his whole life on having this woman. Instead, he has had his heart broken.'

And Tam realised that William was indeed behaving like a broken man, his heart's only function now to keep him alive.

The next morning, after a sleepless night, Tam looked across at William's bed. He moving restlessly; his forehead was hot, perspiring.

A knock at the door revealed Juna, who had also been

anxious about William. She went quickly to his side and confirmed Tam's diagnosis.

'He has a fever, Master Eildor. I will look after him.'

'A bruised jaw could hardly have caused a fever,' Tam said, as he went to join the others.

'Of course not, Tam. I am sure he has taken greater blows than that,' said Marie. 'But maybe a broken heart can't . . .' She shrugged. 'And we know not how that can ever be mended. He has lost the love of his life, his reason for living.'

Halcro had come off watch and nodded sadly when told of William's fever. He would take over command meantime, according to Captain Morham's orders.

Juna was left to take care of him. They all looked in and Linmer said to Tam later that day, seeing her sitting by the bedside, applying cold cloths to his face, 'She seems to know what is needed. She said what he needed most was a day of rest and then he would be well again. Let's hope so.' Linmer sighed. 'First, he loses the love of his life and very soon he will be losing his closest friend.' He regarded Tam sadly, knowing that the time lord must leave them soon or be doomed to stay in this lost world for ever.

Halcro had taken over and pointed out on the map how many sea miles they had to travel before they reached the port of Leith for more supplies, before heading down to Fast Castle to discover whether King James was right in his suspicions that it was the hiding place of the Spanish treasure.

The weather that had been in their favour until they

left Slains now turned its head from them. It seemed to grieve for William, tears shed in the sudden rain. The change was sudden and dramatic as such storms were, but for Captain Morham it had one blessing: it was exactly what was needed to thrust him back into life again. It could not have come at a better time for him to leave the past behind, take command of the *Falcon* and the valuable lives of his passengers and crew, as the sun sank towards a livid purple cloud bank deep on the western horizon.

It was clear that the sea was not going to stay calm much longer. William took his place beside Halcro, firm-footed at the wheel as the sky turned overcast and clouds, carried by a shrill wind, indicated the coming storm. It was a storm even greater than the one they had survived earlier that had threatened their existence in those first days as they turned towards the Scottish north-east coast.

Tam came to his side and William told him that this long swell from the south and the east, this strange humidity that came from both the sky and the glassy surface of the heaving sea as well as the threatening appearance of the veiled sun, might well warn both sailors and landsman of a severance of all natural bonds and a devilish and apoplectic upheaval.

In conclusion he smiled at Tam, who had already decided that this sudden change in the weather gave this particular landsman a strangely awful and foreboding, which added to his fears as the steady increase of the ship's movements turned to violence beneath his feet.

Tam had got used to the majesty of the sea, the beauty of waves and the gentle calm after the recent storm. In a strange way it had inspired his confidence and trust, while he now watched the seamen preparing. There was a sudden demonic squall of rain, a torrent so laden by the end of the middle watch that all their efforts could hardly exaggerate the perils in store. Once the south-easterly gale increased from its first warning blasts at the end of the last dog-watch to a great current of air, the torrent of rain was so strong that William and Halcro had to hold their heads down and cup their mouths.

Tam rushed forward, sliding across the already soaked deck to offer help and was roughly told 'Get below! Take shelter!'

He ignored the plea and found rough shelter on deck as the seas mounted higher and higher and, although not the height of the great Atlantic rollers the two men struggling at the wheel had experienced in their past voyages, they were steeper and, in a way, more formidable. The gale streamed in front of them to race and tear through the *Falcon*'s tops, tall enough to becalm her as she lay there, riding out the storm under a stray staysail.

This was something Tam had learnt she could do superbly well. She might not be a very fast frigate; she might not look dangerous or high bred, but with her top gallant masts struck down on deck and her hatches battened down, she lay to, unconcerned by the whipping of the angry waves upon her side.

Tam observed that she was a remarkably dry vessel too, calm as she climbed the creaming slope of a wave, slipping its roaring top neatly under her bows and travelling smoothly down into its hollow.

He was glad to observe William now fully restored, all the bitterness of a rejected lover cast aside in his true role with all the responsibilities of a sea captain in a storm. Watched in the diffused light of a racing moon, William had the greatest satisfaction noting that his forecast as to his ship's qualities had been fulfilled. He smiled on his passengers, who had been taken aback by the ferocity of the storm and now stood mute, sodden and appalled behind him.

He and Halcro stayed firmly by the wheel until dawn came. The sunrise was swallowed up by the wind, but by half past seven that morning, all that was left of the storm was the swell and a line of clouds low over the distant horizon. The *Falcon* was running diagonally across the swell through the sweeping rain, a little corkscrewing motion with the wind on their beam.

Tam looked upwards to a sky of an unbelievable purity, the air washed so clean that it tasted like wine. He had survived his second sea storm and would always remember those moments of extreme, prostrating terror when he believed he would be hurled overboard and swallowed by a merciless sea.

There was no more trouble from bad weather as the *Falcon* sailed smoothly down the east coast. They finally dropped anchor at the port of Leith where provisions, now much needed, could be bought and Halcro could supervise small repairs to the ship.

Meanwhile, all were delighted at the prospect of seeing the capital of Scotland and spending a little time there, a breathing space from shipboard life. A map of Edinburgh was produced by William, spread on the table and eagerly explored.

After a day in the city all would meet in a convenient tavern, circled by William, who knew the city's main streets well from his earlier days. Together they would then return to the *Falcon* and set forth on the final part of their voyage.

With the *Falcon* anchored at Leith quayside, the passengers made their way across to King's Wark, on the shore facing the harbour. It was of particular interest to Marie, having been designed to serve as a royal residence. Though damaged by English troops, it had survived, a handsome building with a cellar and three chambers.

Marie was intrigued and pointed out the moulded stone doorway decorated with armorial bearings of the Queen Regent Mary of Guise.

'She was my grandmother and she ruled Scotland from here at Leith until my mother came home from France, the dauphin's widow, to be our queen,' she added proudly.

She sighed since anything connected with her mother always drew sad tears.

Owen was glad to share her experiences, her sorrows and her joys, finding it difficult to reconcile the fact that the gracious, elegant and tragic Queen of Scots had shared the same blood with her half-brother, his cruel father, Robert Stewart. He felt particularly incensed that Earl Robert had allowed Marie's father, Lord Bothwell, to be turned away from Orkney, that sanctuary had been so brutally denied him.

As plans were made for departure, Tam considered the situation ironic that he should soon be in Edinburgh again, the destination in his original time plan.

Linmer was elated at the prospect of entering the city. His own part in this mission had been dictated by the Earl. It seemed that King James had heard of the existence of one John Napier. 'A powerful man, greatly respected, he is a scholar and an alchemist, something of a magician, His Majesty has heard.' The Earl frowned for a moment, then continued, 'And I have His Majesty's command that this Napier be sought out and consulted about any way he can help seek out this treasure, since we are given to understand that he is well acquainted with Robert Logan of Fast Castle.'

As a scholar it had been always Linmer's ambition to reach Edinburgh and end his days with some learned men at Trinity College. It functioned both as a community of priests and as a place of shelter for the poor and sick of Edinburgh and had survived the Reformation. He had not informed the others that this was his farewell and that he had no intention of continuing on the voyage mission for the treasure trove.

Considering the frailty of an old man such as Linmer, Tam offered to accompany him into the city.

'It will be a long walk,' he warned, and Linmer smiled.

'I have my staff, so I shall manage well.' But he was pleased by the offer and glad of this last opportunity to spend a few remaining hours with his young time lord friend.

Their journey began accompanied by Zor, who seemed eager as dogs do after some days in the restraint of a sailing ship.

Linmer patted his head. 'You are welcome.' Turning to Tam he said, 'I have heard there are some desolate stretches, unfrequented by humans where we might encounter wolves, so Zor will keep them at bay.'

And so the journey began for Tam and Linmer from the crowded harbour through the little town of Leith, through fields and meadows and waterways, interrupted by drove roads and the occasional dark forest of tall Caledonian pines. They passed through a hamlet of cottages in the shadows of a tall castle, then a church, which suggested a settlement was at hand.

It had been a long walk and when Tam looked at Linmer, he decided the old man had done remarkably well, but must be in need of a rest. And rest there was, in the welcome sight of an inn opposite the church, with a hanging sign moving in the cheerful breeze.

They pushed open the door and were greeted by a genial landlord.

'Aye, sirs, welcome to the Sheep's Heid.' He indicated the date carved in stone above the door and said proudly, 'Been serving good food and ale since it was built in 1360.' He smiled at Zor. 'Aye, sirs, and yer dog is welcome too. A fine animal. He shall have a mutton bone outside.'

This explained the mutton pies and ale Tam and Linmer were to be served, which proved to be a welcome treat after their long walk, while Zor trotted happily after the landlord and the promise of a rare treat for him after the *Falcon*'s meagre rations.

While waiting for refreshment, Tam and Linmer both sniffed and exchanged glances, aware of a strong and unpleasant odour unrelated to sailing ships or mutton pies. It was the strong smell of an abattoir nearby.

Tam's question regarding the inn's name and the smell was phrased tactfully.

The landlord said apologetically, 'We get used to the stink. The sheep are reared in Holyrood Park down yonder and brought here for slaughter. Their skins go to the merchants in the city if that is where you gentlemen are heading.'

Tam asked if it was far. 'Just two or three miles away.'

As they prepared to leave and passed over one of the coins William had provided for refreshment they would need, the landlord wished them 'Godspeed' and said, 'You take the same road as our dear queen did by the base of that huge mountain on your left, which is known as Arthur's Seat, then walk through the park where the sheep are grazing. You won't see the Nor Loch in the distance, but the park will lead you to Holyroodhouse and up a steep street a mile long through the Netherbow port of the city. On a high rock you'll see Edinburgh's castle.'

Tam was intrigued as they walked according to the landlord's directions and knew vaguely from the ancient literature of Planet Earth tales of Scotland's magnificent heritage.

As they walked in the shadow of Arthur's Seat, Linmer said, 'Such a strange name.'

'There are many legends concerning King Arthur in Britain,' Tam replied, and as they looked across the rock-strewn slopes to its summit that resembled not a king's head but a lion couchant, his information was probably more recent and up to date than Linner's. Tam went on to explain, 'Arthur's Seat is an extinct volcano about two million years old with its adjoining Salisbury Crags all formed from the same rock on which Edinburgh Castle stands. The name has aroused many myths through the ages, once regarded as Camelot and the home of King Arthur.'

Linmer was finding the uphill climb wearying, and Tam indicated a nearby bounder where they might rest.

'All places have their mythical connection, but this one is an interesting legend. A shepherd boy rounding up a stray sheep stumbled on the entrance to a cave where the King was sleeping with his knights and their hounds. At his hand on the table, a horn lay in readiness to awaken his knights and ride out should Britain need his call to arms.'

They were both aware of a change in Zor since the old volcano had come into view. He was no longer happy to remain at Linmer's side, but ran ahead and his expression was one of great excitement, as if he had been long awaiting this moment, listening and paying particular attention to this legend, staring up at the hill in a manner of expectation,

'The less romantic explanation is that the name is a corruption of the Gaelic "Ard-na-said" implying Hill of the Arrows or Archer's Seat.'

Zor returned to Linmer's side and the doctor placed an arm around the wolf-dog, then looked at Tam intently.

'Is our place on earth?' And before he could respond Linmer continued, 'We both know that our place is not on Planet Earth, and not in this century.' He shook his head. 'We both know, Tam Eildor, that a puff of wind could blow us away and all we have keeping us here is a switch on a time machine. We don't belong in this century and neither does Zor. He knows that, don't you?' He patted Zor's head and was rewarded by that oddly smiling look. Turning again to Tam, he asked, 'Have you not noticed the way he has been watching Arthur's Seat, ever since you told that tale about King Arthur?'

That was true and Tam observed again what had always been there: Zor and Linmer belonged together, in the same time. And that had always been obvious from the moment Zor pulled him from the sea in Orkney.

Zor was watching Linmer closely and Tam knew that the strange wolf-dog understood every word the old man uttered.

Linmer smiled. 'Yes, Tam Eildor, I see you understand this is no ordinary animal, but a creature in the shape of a wolf-dog with superhuman intelligence, who belongs to our time, yours and mine, whenever that is. We read each other's thoughts; it has always been as if we share one mind and if I was ever in danger, he would know to warn me.'

Exchanging with Zor what Tam recognised as a look of understanding, Linmer said, 'He is telling me something.' He sighed. 'He has come home. He knew from the moment we walked this path that it is where he must leave us.'

'You mean he is going to die?'

Linmer shrugged. 'Perhaps, for no one knows how old he is. He wants to be with his own kind, hopefully for a new life. We came to a parting of our ways when the *Falcon* landed at Leith. The moment was waiting for Zor, and we must go on alone now, Tam.'

He looked at Zor and said, 'He understands.'

Tam understood, too, for Zor always belonged to Linmer who went on, 'I set him to take care of Marie, but she won't miss him. She has Owen now and he is her whole world. He knew I needed his presence on our travels. He is nothing to the others, but he saved your life, Tam Eildor. You were special. There was a bond.' To Zor he instructed, 'Go, my friend. Your time with me is ended. Go!'

Again, Tam watched that look of understanding that would have been put into words if Zor had been given that gift. Now, he leant close to Linmer and, with a final wag of his tail, turned headed up the hill without a backward glance. Tam felt this must have been a dreadful moment for Linmer. He could think of nothing to say as the hill finally absorbed Zor.

'There's no need for concern, Tam. If, when our day in Edinburgh is ended, he has changed his mind and wants to return, he will be waiting for us.'

Again, he sighed. 'He was glad to leave Orkney; he never expected to see it again, but he knows this is his lost world. I have to let him go for now, as there would be no place for him in the Edinburgh that I will live in, for a few years anyway. Though hopefully we will meet again.'

Tam didn't understand , only some of what Linmer said made sense. Zor had always been Linmer's and it was not death that was parting them now but the unseen powers of the other world to which Linmer, Zor and himself belonged.

As they walked along the road leading to Edinburgh, Tam realised that Linmer was carrying a heavy heart, his steps slow and faltering, as if losing Zor had suddenly aged him. The road was busy with passing traffic, but the driver of a cart laden with farm produce stopped next to them. The driver leant over and said cheerfully, 'Want a ride into the town, old man?'

Linmer smiled gratefully and the driver leapt down to give him a helping hand. 'You too, young sir.'

There was little chance of conversation and Tam watched Linmer, whose head had sunk on to his chest. The doctor made no movement apart from an occasional glance back along the road they were leaving, as if Zor might be following.

At last, the walls of the city came in sight and they drove in through the Netherbow Port, the great gateway giving access from Edinburgh into the south and beyond to the Borders.

Tam thanked the driver for his kindness, deciding on rest and refreshment at a nearby tavern, considering Linmer's melancholic state, before facing another uphill climb.

Half an hour later, after receiving careful directions, they were on their way to Merchiston Tower. Linmer had recovered enough to tell Tam, 'The theory is that Robert Logan coveted the fertile brain of John Napier for purposes of his own regarding hidden treasure.'

This residence of John Napier stood a little to the south of Edinburgh. From its battlement walk, for it had originally been built for defence, Napier could admire the signature in the sky inscribed by the town's roofs at sunset and salute its bold castle rock and ramparts in the morning.

The girdle of the Lowlands was close enough to touch, with all Lothian towards the North Sea visible at a glance. By raising an eye he could take in the coast of Fife backed by green hill, wood and pasture on the same line of vision, the blue mountain barrier of the Highlands, almost the whole jewelled country compressed into a single image. At night the stairway up to the turret room and the open battlement became a tour with his mighty telescope to a conference with the stars.

While Tam and Linmer waited on the steps of this impressive building, the door was opened by a servant who took their names, and as they stood now indecisive about their reception, a tall, distinguished-looking scholar in long robe and velvet bonnet, undoubtedly John Napier, appeared and Linmer bowed, producing the Earl's document authorising that this visit concerned a royal command.

John Napier's smile and dismissive gesture indicated that he had many such royal summons. He looked at them and said, 'If you will follow me,' then led the way up a spiral of steep stairs with occasional landings to a turret room in the high tower. There Linmer noticed with delight a powerful telescope directed over the city as well as many of the instruments used by astronomers.

Tam knew from his history books that Napier was also a mathematician and physicist, reputed to be a magician dabbling in alchemy and necromancy. Linmer followed Napier to a table, which was overcrowded with books and papers.

There Napier pushed the papers aside and proudly indicated his present work,

'A Plaine Discovery of the Whole Revelation of St John'. As Linmer apologised for this interruption by unexpected visitors, Napier shook his head, waving the apology aside.

'This I believe to be my most important publication, based on the Book of Revelations. It's a mathematical analysis by which I hope to predict the date of the Apocalypse.' Tam knew that Napier was now in his late thirties and, despite being a tall imposing presence with thick dark hair and fine eyes, a heavy beard made him appear older. Though Tam accepted this was the middle age of a time, when few survived past their late forties, regarded as old age.

Napier seemed delighted to have visitors and invited them to take a seat, while a servant was summoned to bring wine. Tam could see by Linmer's rapt expression that after his long, lonely years in Orkney, he had at last found a soulmate.

'Life was not easy when I came to Merchiston. Neighbours accused me of being a sorcerer. The rumour was, I suspected, based on the servants' gossip. All the hours I spent in my study here with the door locked saying that I was not to be disturbed, was interpreted as me being in league with the Devil and learning the black art.'

Pausing, he laughed and raised a glass of wine. 'These rumours were not helped when, after I discovered that various items were missing, being stolen and sold, I used my pet rooster to catch the thief. I told the servants to go into a darkened room and pat the rooster I had coloured black by covering it with soot.' Again, he laughed and said, 'I claimed that my rooster would crow if touched by the one who stole my property. When they emerged considerably shaken, I inspected their hands to find the thief was the one with clean hands. He had been too afraid to touch the rooster guessing it would crow and proclaim his guilt, so he was dismissed immediately.'

Their host was obviously enjoying company, which Tam suspected was probably quite a rare event as he went on.

'Another act which must have mystified the local residents, and was probably attributed to my association with the Devil, was the trouble I had with pigeons descending in hordes and eating grain from my estate. I had an idea and it worked. I caught them by strewing grain laced with alcohol through the field and captured those too drunk to fly away. I am fond of animals; they have a great deal more intelligence than we humans rate them.'

Tam thought of Zor as Napier sighed. 'I miss my pet rooster. Some years ago I had a magpie who could speak.'

Tam looked at Linmer, the same thought passing through their minds. Was this a home for Mags once the voyage was over? They suspected that Owen would be embarrassed by Marie taking her to Alnwick with them.

Before they left, Linmer apologised again for interrupting his writing, but Napier seemed unconcerned, happy to share more details about his project.

As they walked down steep stairs with Napier in the lead, Tam nudged Linmer and mouthed, 'Fast Castle' It was as well he did so for Linmer, still in a glow of what had been a supremely fascinating visit, had forgotten the main object of their visit to establish some link with Napier and the treasure trove.

Shaking hands at the door, Napier asked what plans they had for a future stay in Edinburgh.

Both shook their heads, said it was a brief visit and Linmer said boldly, 'The ship's captain thought we might go down the coast and have a look at Fast Castle.' Napier merely smiled vaguely. Linmer indicated the Earl's document and continued, 'As a magician, sir, have you heard aught of a treasure trove there?'

Napier, with one hand on the door, smiled and said, 'I

am acquainted with Robert Logan. We have matters of business in common.'

And with that they had to be satisfied.

In the ground floor chamber, a fine room with vaulted ceiling, farewells were exchanged.

'What are your plans, Dr Linmer? Do you intend returning to Edinburgh?' asked Napier.

'I am intending to stay, sir. My plan is to approach Trinity College for possible admittance.'

Napier looked at him sharply. 'If you should change your mind, doctor, there would always be a place for you here. I am sorely in need, and have been for some time, for someone of your high intellect to assist me in my experiments. Your experience would be invaluable.'

He watched them go, wishing he had had an opportunity to learn more about Dr Erasmus Linmer's young companion. He was a strange fellow who did not quite fit the pattern of present-day youth. Those wide, luminous eyes reminded him of a saint's statue in St Giles' Church before the Reformation had put an end to Catholicism and forcibly smashed holy relics.

CHAPTER TWENTY-FIVE

Soon they were to rejoin at the meeting place as agreed by William, the White Hart Inn in the Grassmarket.

Inside the inn, their fellow passengers greeted the safe arrival of Tam and Linmer, all eager to share their accounts of this new experience. Zor's absence was explained by Linmer that he was taking a chance to explore the fresh air, an explanation casually accepted without comment since they all knew that Zor was no usual dog. While their orders for food and wine were placed, they took comfortable seats by the window overlooking the busy street of marketable goods.

William had been busy in the last few hours and to everyone's relief and delight had made arrangements with one of his merchants for them to accompany the cart carrying provisions for the *Falcon* back to Leith.

They would meet at sundown at the Netherbow

Port. 'We still have time in hand,' he said to all, before turning to Tam. 'I have made some changes on board. The *Falcon* will be setting sail with less crew. Our valued cook will remain with us as well as the two Flett brothers who are excellent sailors. Some of the others wish to return to Orkney as they have wives and children there and are fearful of the Earl's displeasure before he learns that they abandoned the *Falcon* and the remainder of the voyage to Fast Castle. They will wait at Leith for the next merchant vessel sailing to Kirkwall or Stromness, while those tempted to seek their fortunes according to rumour, readily available in a rich city like Edinburgh, will stay on land.'

A captain, a boson and three sailors. It did not sound encouraging to Tam and, looking at his expression, William said, 'We will manage fine, if the weather holds.'

If the weather holds, thought Tam, as William added, 'It is only a few miles down the coast to Fast Castle.'

They left the Grassmarket for the West Bow, the steep street where the narrow road was shadowed by projecting galleries from tight-knit houses with overhanging upper stories forming the main route to the castle. Tam reflected that although the journey to the city had been a pleasurable outing for Marie, Owen and Juna, he was glad of William's arrangement to return to Leith on a cart, since walking back to the ship might be difficult for an old and rather frail man like Dr Linmer, if he decided to return with them rather than accept Napier's offer.

Their walk took them near St Giles, the city's most important church. It had once been lavishly decorated with statues and stained glass, housing the altars of then local crafts guilds. Marie, who had been baptised and brought up in the old faith, as had Owen, decided that a candle should be lit and prayers said for their journey.

The others followed her into the dim and vast interior where Tam was suddenly aware that this was the first time he had been in such a vast religious building, devoted to the presence of the Almighty God of the Planet Earth, who had become the Master Builder of his own time. He felt awed, the need to say something – to pray, if that was the word – for the certainty that this Almighty God and the Master Builder were one and the same.

He knelt with the rest of them next to Marie.

As she bowed her head and genuflected, she whispered, 'A Requiem Mass should have been said for my dear mother. Jesus and the Virgin Mary would have greeted her soul in Heaven for even in her last moment on earth awaiting the executioner's sword, their names were on her lips. She never in all her trials wavered in the true faith.'

At her side William had his head bowed in prayer, remembering his own upbringing and his devout grandmother while Owen, whose family did lip service to a God whose commandments they constantly broke, put up a prayer for forgiveness.

They stood up again, dusted down their knees and walked down the nave to the unadorned high altar where the empty niches once held holy statues, before leaving the sacred place. Thence to the Cowgate. According to William, acting as their guide, it was one of the most prosperous parts of the city and Tam observed that the houses were not packed together so closely as in the streets they had left.

'This is where the nobility and chief men of the city reside,' William continued. 'Fifty years ago money was left for a hospital and a chapel at its western end, dedicated to Mary Magdalene.' So saying, he hurried ahead. St Giles had been enough and he didn't wish to delay for yet another religious establishment.

As they continued their walk, Tam was observing signs of growing weariness among his fellow passengers who had started off so enthusiastically. It had been a well-packed day for all on rough streets, as few were cobblestoned, and he was particularly concerned for the old doctor. He therefore applauded William's idea for negotiating a cart for the return to the ship.

When he mentioned this to Linmer, he was rewarded with a smile and Linmer indicated the sturdy staff he had carried throughout the voyage, especially useful and always carried for safety on the *Falcon*'s swaying deck.

As they stopped to sit on a ruined wall and admire the view of the castle, the doctor smiled and, in answer to William's questions, he sighed.

'Indeed, I am a little weary. It has been a long but happy day and, as an old man, I am grateful for your consideration. I should not like to be a burden, but I am only going one way; no return journey with you, this time.'

Puzzled, they regarded him in astonishment and concern. Was he feeling ill?

He laughed and, stretching his arms wide, he said, 'This is my destination; this is as far as I ever intended to travel. I have always wanted to see Edinburgh, having heard much about it through literature. It is a scholar's paradise, so I intend to stay here. Hopefully I may be accepted at Trinity College, one of the great houses of learning. As you see, I have left my days as an alchemist for ever,' he indicated the small sack he carried, 'and have brought only what will be necessary for my new life.

'You will have to continue your voyage to Fast Castle without me, Captain Morham, although that will not be a great loss.' He added to Tam, in an excited whisper, 'Though Trinity College was my destination before we met John Napier. Now, I may change my mind.'

Pausing, he looked up at the sky and said to Marie, 'I may have found a home for your faithful Mags. John Napier, who Tam and I have just visited, is very anxious to have an intelligent bird to replace his pet rooster.'

'Excellent,' said William, 'if you are agreeable, sister, we can put her in my parrot cage and the next messenger into Edinburgh will deliver her to him.'

Marie smiled sadly. Mags had found herself a home on the masthead and seemed quite comfortable on her lofty perch. Although the sea birds avoided her on the *Falcon*, she was afraid the gulls at the port of Leith might not respect her. Tam did not doubt that this magical bird could deal with any intruders Napier might receive.

Marie sighed. 'I shall miss her, but I am glad her future is secured.'

* * *

'That is a relief,' Owen put in, having given some deep thought to how a pet magpie with a taste for bright gems might be received by his mother's family. 'I could not visualise her flying alongside us when we journey on to Northumberland. When we return from Fast Castle,' he added 'and I have delivered some kind of message for the King's satisfaction, we will hire a coach for Alnwick.' At the next stopping place, before they reached the Netherbow Port and waited for the cart to collect them, they discussed what plans each had after Fast Castle and the unlikely prospect of finding the Spanish treasure, which none of them seriously believed existed.

Owen and Marie talked of a future they believed was waiting at Alnwick Castle. William smiled vaguely at Tam, having no idea of what he planned.

'I hope to return with Halcro to Orkney. There is some plan afoot for us to take the ship at Leith.' Putting it into words made Tam shudder, realising that unless he was very careful and very lucky, he might be in danger of ending up like Dr Linmer, a lost traveller in time.

Their attention turned to Juna, who was sitting quietly, saying nothing. They had forgotten that she, too, had a future.

'What will you do?' William asked, though he suspected he knew the answer.

She smiled. 'As I've said before, I will try and find a ship going to the New World and find my people again.'

Doubtful looks were exchanged. She still obviously never thought that money would be required and both

William and Owen said together, 'We will provide the fare, for you have served us perfectly on our voyage.'

Marie leant over and, putting an arm about the girl said, 'If you wish you can come with us to Alnwick instead.' She darted a quick look at Owen, who nodded and smiled enthusiastically. Marie having a companion was a splendid idea.

William said little, since he had already told them of his intention to sell the *Falcon* when their mission ended and Owen had delivered the message concerning the treasure in person to the King. Tam looked at his sad expression and guessed that he had not yet produced any substitute future to replace this, since his heart had been broken at the Mearns. The faces of the others revealing their compassion.

Observing their concern, William shrugged and said, 'There are other ships; there is the whole of Europe to explore. I should have done that in the normal way, after my granddam died and I left Morham, but somehow,' he paused sadly, 'that was overlooked in my family's eagerness to be rid of me.'

The sun was low in the sky and cast a perfect sunset as they emerged and joined the cart loaded with provisions.

It was time to say farewell to Dr Linmer. He had been so much a part of their lives that all were grieved that their ways were to part. Perhaps secretly all were having doubts, in particular Tam after their conversation, how they would deal with the rest of the voyage with fewer crew members and the dangers that could await at Fast Castle even for the young and strong,

There was little chance of conversation and less for comfort in the cart with its two horses. On the road, by the base of Arthur's Seat, there was no sign of Zor. Tam thought again of that sad parting and how he would miss the wise old man. The thoughts of the other passengers were turned to Leith and what lay ahead for the *Falcon*'s last voyage with its captain.

Aboard the *Falcon* once more, minus Linmer and Zor, Marie said a tearful farewell to Mags, watching William place her in his parrot cage with a delivery cart bound for Edinburgh and on to Napier.

Mags cawed woefully at her beloved mistress, who tried to restrain her tears. It was not a cheerful evening and they were glad to set sail at daybreak, relieved that they were now on the last part of the voyage, with the ultimate goal was in sight and their new futures ahead.

Next morning, a few miles down the coast, they sailed on a sea as smooth as silk. The *Falcon*'s sails fluttered gently in a sunny breeze until at last the grim outline of Fast Castle came into view and Halcro fired the gunshot to signal their arrival.

'They awaited some return signal and hoped of a welcoming reception, unlike that found at the Mearns. At last, William handed Tam the map and, having found the headland he was looking for, carefully negotiated the *Falcon* in the direction of a massive cathedral-like cave. It was the only entrance that opened into the grim crag, growing closer as a stark tower with an appendage of domestic buildings arising from its summit.

The others looked anxiously over the ship's rail into the depths of a deep water harbour in front of the cave, partially screened by a large sea stack, identified by Tam on the map as the Wheat Stack. Beyond, there was another large pinnacle of rock, which William considered most probably the harbour that had caused the castle to be built here originally.

'It has a strange name,' said Marie.

'And it's not very welcoming,' said Owen.

'Faux Castle was its original name before it became wider known as Fast,' William explained. 'It was built as a defence tower and that, I think, implied in one word that its true business had once been associated with some signal treachery.'

The harbour was obviously well used, or had been, for despite the initial appearance, there was ample room for the *Falcon* to drop anchor. Juna had elected to stay on the ship saying she had much sewing to do, but her real reason was the approach to the dark, forbidding castle above terrified her.

Still, they waited in the heavy silence, curious to know more about Robert Logan and what sort of reception they might expect.

Owen asked William, 'What kind of a man is he?'

'A man of property. His lands lie between Holyroodhouse and the Port of Leith and also take in the great expanse of Holyrood Park. His larger inheritance stretches to the Borders and the wild coastal strip of the Lammermuirs.' He paused. 'And his territory terminates at the cliff edge here—'

Owen interrupted, 'Including this grim place that thrusts its mass beyond the cliffs into the North Sea.'

Now creeping doubts that their voyage had been in vain assailed them and they continued to wait, fearing the worst. The castle far above them seemed deserted, falling into ruin, thought Tam. Suddenly a servant appeared and indicated the flight of rough stone steps.

It was a stiff climb and, as Owen helped Marie up, Tam was thankful that Linmer was not one of the party. At last, they reached the top and emerged into a wide courtyard. As they gathered, the servant was waiting.

But as William rushed forward and knelt to kiss her hand, they saw that this was no female servant in rough working attire, who had indicated their passage up the cliff, but was undoubtedly Lady Logan, William's Aunt Janet.

Giving them a moment to take in the surroundings and recover their breaths, looking up the coast towards the capital they saw a line of gentle cliffs and farmland stretching far into a misty inland horizon. Lady Logan led them across the courtyard singularly less forbidding than the view from below suggested.

Opening the heavy oak door into a great chamber with a vaulted ceiling and a handsome fireplace, she invited them to be seated at the huge oak table, with places already laid, indicating that they were expected, as a manservant appeared with goblets of wine and William proceeded with the introductions.

Lady Logan was particularly interested to meet Lady Marie Hepburn, an interest well reciprocated when Marie was informed, 'Your mother, Queen Mary, stayed here on several occasions and found us convenient as a discreet channel for communications with France.' Pausing, she added sadly, 'After her abdication and imprisonment it became a bolt hole for the northern English Catholic earls.'

'No doubt my grandfather was one of them,' Owen said grimly. When it was Tam's turn to bow, introduced by William as 'My good friend, an Edinburgh lawyer,' Tam had made already made some rapid observations regarding the present company who were all kin. It seemed quite extraordinary to realise that these persons with royal blood were all closely related and gathered together under one roof.

A sulky, rather plain young girl had joined them and said not a word, eyes firmly fixedly on her plate. Lady Logan had told them she was her daughter, Jean, but the girl made no move beyond a weary shrug to acknowledge, as far as she was concerned, the unimportance of their presence.

Her mother's lips tightened in repressed anger. This revealed to Tam something of the domestic pattern emerging clearly from the shabby gowns worn by both females in a noble household, where a modicum of fashionable elegance was to be expected on display as a wealthy landowner's womenfolk. Here there was not even a jewelled headdress nor a rope of pearls. Ringless hands hinted that this was not a happy family and that the baron was cautious with his wealth.

Where was Robert Logan?

Clearly the same thought had occurred to William who, looking around, asked politely as the dishes of cold meats were set before them, 'Uncle Robert? Are we not to await him?'

'No,' was the sharp reply. 'I have not the least idea where he is at present.' Her shrug was eloquent and told Tam she did not care either as she added, 'He does not favour his family with information in such matters as his whereabouts.' She looked sharply at her daughter Jean with a hostile glance hostile. 'It could be that he is arranging a match for our daughter, with some suitably noble family.'

Tam took in the girl and her shudder of distaste, as he reflected once more on the miserable life of daughters in the upper classes. If they survived infancy, which claimed so many children, they were regarded as mere negotiable financial assets by their parents.

He looked at William, desperately trying to put the conversation on an even keel, though Logan's essential presence was lacking.

While an attempt at polite table conversation was taking place, Owen was no longer concerned with the whereabouts of the treasure, if ever he had been. Lady Logan recalled a past meeting with William in which she mentioned his grandmother.

'A dear lady. I remember visiting Morham when we were in Edinburgh and meeting you, William.' She paused and touched his hand. 'I don't suppose you remember that. You were very young.'

William laughed. 'I was six, aunt, and I remember

perfectly. Uncle Robert kindly gave me three gold coins. As you can imagine, I had never had such a fortune thrust into my hands and was bewildered by having such generosity bestowed on a small boy.'

When they left later and were rowing back to the ship, Tam remarked to William on his remarkable memory.

William smiled and said, 'It was like a fortune, those coins. I thought of all the things I might buy with such a treasure.' While Tam was concluding that twenty years had turned a very rich man into a mean and greedy one judging by the state of his family and unhappy wife at the castle they had just left, William went on, 'I felt guilty and ashamed that I had been too taken aback to even thank him politely, even when my grandmother laughed and assured me that I might have some problems spending this small bounty. She said, "But it need not worry you. You can have anything you wish to buy from me. I will keep these safe for you."'

Rubbing his chin, he smiled at the fond memory of that day. 'She took the coins and put them into a red velvet purse.' He frowned. 'It was trimmed with pearls. I expect it is still in the chest where I keep personal things, especially ones I have a sentimental regard for.'

He thought for a moment. 'I think I shall give it to Juna. The purse would make a nice present, a thank you for all she has done for us.'

The meal had ended without the presence of Logan. With no excuse to linger, or to receive the vital information they were hoping for, Owen said, 'This whole voyage would have been just a waste of time and effort, except that it helped Marie escape and made our future together possible. I will have nothing to tell His Majesty. We are not one whit further on that matter than when we left Orkney,' he whispered to Tam, half listening to William tell Lady Logan that sailing down the coast with friends, he thought it would be pleasant to look in on his aunt and uncle before returning to Edinburgh where he intended to sell the *Falcon*.

Lady Logan smiled. 'I am so glad you found us at home, William. Jean and I spend most of our time at Dowlaw, the home farm up the road.' She suppressed a shiver. 'The castle here tends to be chilly, and we have few reasons for guests these days, or a royal progress,' she added, with a smile at Marie.

'I have loved meeting you. It has been the greatest pleasure,' Marie answered.

Lady Logan then gave a deep curtsey. 'Your Royal Highness—'

'No, please!'

But Lady Logan ignored the interruption, shook her head and continued 'Your Royal Highness, your dear mother would have been proud of you. God rest her soul.'

The climb down the steep steps to where the *Falcon* waited was easier than the upward climb and, as Tam stood at the wheel beside William, they both looked up at the castle. As the ship negotiated its careful way back into the sea beyond the harbour, Tam was not sorry to shed the bad energy that the sad visit had given him. There was more than a touch of lingering evil of past tragedies and blood shed, the calls of the dying mixed with the seabirds' cries and waves thundering madly against that inscrutable castle on the cliff edge.

William looked at his friend's face and said, 'I did not like it much either. It's not a place I would choose for more than a fleeting visit. The proud vaunt was that twelve men within its walls could withstand the siege of an army. Dr Linmer told me that it has an evil reputation, a shameful record as a wreckers' castle.'

The *Falcon* loomed above them and, climbing the rope ladder while the small boat was hauled aboard, William gave orders to make full sail and head into the southerly wind that would take them back to Leith.

CHAPTER TWENTY-SIX

They arrived back in Leith in the glow of an evening with just a touch of twilight in its mellow beauty, but also a touch of melancholy too. As they prepared to take final leave of each other they had shared much joy in their companionship, although a failure in their main mission, to discover the location of lost treasure.

Whilst William dealt with merchants and found a shipping agent who would be available tomorrow morning for the sale of his ship, the crew went about making the *Falcon* look its very best, scrubbing decks, cleaning timbers, all to give the best appeal for a buyer and the best price for Captain Morham.

Halcro had accompanied William, who was looking for a merchant vessel heading for Orkney with passages for himself and Tam. Tam did not care where exactly he landed, as long as it was not in the same manner as his original arrival on the beach. His return would seem desolate without Linmer, Zor, or Marie. Most of all he would lose William Hepburn for ever.

The friends were all too tired and dispirited to sit around the great table for a final drink together before they went off to their beds on the *Falcon* for the last time. Tam felt that he would miss the gentle rhythmic creak of the timbers, the soothing sway of his bunk as well as William's snoring in the opposite cot.

He knew how much he would miss this friend. Would he even remember him? That seemed unlikely as memories of time travel were non-retentive and quickly erased when one returned to their own time. But not completely, the thin gossamer strands of his memory of Marie Seton, a great love lost, still remained. Would he ever meet a woman he could love for ever and yield to the temptation to stay, as Linmer had done, in some past century?

At least Linmer had one problem solved and a new life in Napier's tower in Edinburgh.

He thought of the others, of Marie and Owen, and realised he would never know the ending of their journey. He would always wonder whether they had been well-received by the Percy family in Northumberland and lived happy ever after, as this was unlikely to be recorded in any historic records. And what of Juna? Would she go with them to remain by Marie's side, or would she journey across the sea searching for her home?

He closed his eyes and as always when he opened them again, he had no indication of time passing. It was the next morning. In the great cabin next door, assembled around the table for the last time, they all broke their fast. Owen and Marie were beaming in high excitement.

'At the shipping office, there was a message for the ship. For one Owen Stewart,' William reported.

'It was from my uncle, Earl Percy at Alnwick,' said Owen, unable to contain his delight. 'They had got my message, which I sent before we left Kirkwall, and said that all the family would be waiting to welcome us.'

'Isn't that wonderful?' said Marie.

It was indeed to Tam, who thought that of any message carried hundreds of miles over land by only the means of a fast horse or , if one was lucky and could afford it, a coach. Even with four wheels instead of four legs, considering the hazards of natural travel such as robbers, wolves and non-existent roads, for a coach to safely reach its destination and repeat the same to bring a reply was like magic to him..

'Did you get a buyer?' Tam asked William, who smiled and shook his head.

'I had an offer, but I have changed my mind about selling.'

They gazed at him in astonishment, with quick thoughts in all their minds whether this indicated a regrettable return to his former life of piracy.

He smiled. 'I am keeping the *Falcon*, but will be taking her to the New World.' He bowed gently towards Juna, silent as always, who smiled softly like one who has a precious secret to conceal. And suddenly Tam knew that her happiness related to William, as he leant over and touched her hand.

'We are sailing to the New World and I am taking Juna back to her tribe – as my wife,' he added gently.

Owen and Marie, with exclamations of delight, rose from the table to hug and wish them joy, which in William's case was richly deserved for having his heart so recently broken by betrayal.

Tam joined in the congratulations, realising what they all knew already, that Juna was deeply in love with William. It was a love at first sight when he had accepted her aboard as a stowaway.

He looked at her and said, 'We all have much to be grateful to you for. You took care of me when I was sick, you have made clothes for us; even, I understand, a suitable gown for Lady Marie's appearance in Alnwick Castle.'

So saying, he reached in his pocket and held up out a red velvet purse trimmed with pearls. 'This is for you, Juna, with all our gratitude. It belonged to my grandmother.' He grinned. 'This is the very same purse my aunt talked about concerning her visit to Morham when my uncle so generously gave me a gift of three coins. They are still there – listen.'

He tipped them out onto the table and said, 'So here they are and it gives me the greatest pleasure to give them to you, my dear, to spend as you wish—'

Tam was examining the coins. 'Not these ones, William. She won't be any better able to spend them. Nor will any of us.'

Puzzled, they turned to him. 'Why not?'

'Because these aren't current coinage of the realm. These are Spanish coins.' Tam held them up to the light. 'See, they bear King Philip's head.'

And at that there was a sudden flash of understanding. Robert Logan, always unwilling to part with money, had surprised all by this flash of generosity o f giving three coins to the child William. Except that they were useless to spend in Scotland.

But what was most important came from Owen, holding one for examination.Owen was laughing. 'Don't you see? This is our answer. The coins must have been part of King Philip's invasion fund, and as such I can give them to His Majesty with the assurance that these may well be evidence of the treasure's whereabouts. I doubt that my father will be delighted with this news or the fact that no reward money will be forthcoming.'

Leaning over, he took Marie's hand. 'But this is the best possible news for us. We are free of Earl Robert, for ever.'

'And your brothers, to say nothing of Patrick.' Marie shuddered at the nightmare memory of that intended marriage.

William stood up. 'Shall we adjourn to the royal court and get it over with? I think on this occasion, a coach is needed.'

One was available, having dropped off passengers with their cabin trunks for a ship about to sail. Marie would go with Owen, curious to meet the King who, like William, was also her half-brother. She would wear the brocade gown that Juna had made from William's mass of materials accumulated and forgotten from his piracy days.

'I am so happy for you and William.' Marie sighed as Juna pinned up her hair. 'But I know I shall never find another so very talented as you, as well as such a trusted friend.'

In the coach, William outlined his plan with Juna at his side. He wished to give her another chance before they sailed to explore the luckenbooths in the mile-long street leading up to the castle, having decided that the *Falcon* would benefit from a woman's touch on their voyage across the Atlantic. Halcro had been given the task of finding at short notice sailors in Leith willing to make up the crew, as well as persuading those who had left ship at the port to return for this exciting new voyage.

William had declined Owen's suggestion that he should accompany them to meet the King.

'I fear that as the son of Lord Bothwell I would be an unhappy reminder of past days, so we will leave you here and return to the ship.' He looked at Tam. 'Halcro has booked passage for you both I believe. When Owen has delivered his message we will have one last meeting on the ship, drink to our futures and say our farewells.'

Owen said, 'It is likely that this might be our farewell. When our royal court mission is ended, we may not return to the *Falcon* but head straight on to Alnwick.'

This was not unexpected for Tam had noticed that

Marie had accepted a small trunk packed with her few possessions from Juna.

'Are we to part now and never meet again, brother?' Marie asked William. She stretched out her hand to William almost tearfully, aware now that decisions had been made and such a meeting was unlikely, despite William's reassuring smile.

'Never say never, dear sister. Only the good Lord knows what lies ahead for all of us.'

Owen was getting anxious, frowning and biting his lip nervously. He had hoped William would accompany him to the royal audience. In desperate need for some support, he turned to Tam.

'Will you be my squire?'

When Tam looked doubtful, Owen explained eagerly that the King would consider it strange that the son of the Earl of Orkney was unattended by at least one gentleman of his court.

Tam was still uncertain, but could hardly refuse and thought it would be an interesting episode of his time travel to see the royal court of Holyrood, before the return voyage on the merchant vessel to Orkney with Halcro and then back to his own time.

As the royal gates to the imposing palace swung open to admit them, Marie and William knew that this was their moment of farewell. As they dismounted from the coach, embraces were exchanged and Marie fought back ready tears at leaving the brother she had only recently discovered and the girl who would be her good sister.

The hardest parting for William was losing Tam, who through the passing years had remained as William's hero. Now he knew there was no likelihood of ever seeing again the man he had so long revered and respected, who would within minutes be gone out of his life for ever, leaving only the remembrance of how he had relished those days they had shared aboard the *Falcon*, the close friendship that neither he nor Tam had ever experienced before.

Stepping out of the coach, the two men embraced and William said, although he knew it was not in the shades of destiny, 'Farewell, dear friend. Until we meet again.' And taking the arm of Juna, being wished a tearful 'Godspeed' by Marie, the two headed quickly out of the gate and onto the mile-long street into the city.

William had seen Juna and Tam speak briefly, their heads together as if there was some understanding between his friend and the girl from the New World. Juna would one day tell him she had known more of Tam Eildor than any suspected, had recognised him as a time lord, for her father was a shaman and could see far into the future, a gift she shared.

CHAPTER TWENTY-SEVEN

Owen was asked to provide identification at the entrance to the royal reception chamber and produced the document with the seal of his father, the Earl of Orkney. There were no further questions. As far as the questioner was concerned, the identities of the man and woman with him were of no importance and the door was opened into a noisy gallery of many petitioners, for an audience with the King.

Guessing that many had already been waiting since daybreak, and expecting a long delay amongst such an army of suppliants, they were surprised at an order to make way as the figure of King James shuffled into view.

He was a similar age to Marie, but looked much older than his years and certainly much older than his cousin Owen and his half-sister. But first sight impressions were not reliable and Tam remembered from reading earth history that this king would come to rule over Scotland and England, also translating the Bible from Latin into English.

As His Majesty progressed slowly down the line, leaning on the arm of his latest favourite, bonnets were doffed, heads bowed and curtseys dipped.

Owen whispered to Tam, 'If we are separated by this crowd, we will perhaps see you later. If not—'

He got no further, suddenly aware that the King had stopped beside him and was making a gesture for the crowd of courtiers to make way.

'You brought me good news, sir,' he said, eagerly indicating the document Owen had brought. 'The information I have long awaited about the Spanish gold.'

Mention of gold of any kind made him emotional. His eyes glistened excitedly. 'We will talk of it over yonder.' He pointed to the door leading outside into the much-needed fresh air, away from odours heavy with the press of unwashed humanity, of sweat and heavy perfumes.

A few steps behind, Tam and Marie followed them into the gardens shadowed by the abbey, enhanced by the smell of summer flowers and the trilling harmonies of birdsong.

The King led the way, shaking off his favourite's arm, with his courtiers scuttling along behind to keep pace with him, hanging onto their feathered hats in the refreshing breeze. Despite his small stature he walked exceedingly fast and stopped suddenly at a small arbour, gestured to dismiss the now sulking favourite and, ignoring Tam and Marie, turned to Owen.

'What have ye for me? Out with it,' he demanded eagerly.

Bowing, Owen laid the three gold coins into the King's outstretched hand. His response could only be described as a snarl of disappointment as he threw them to the ground.

'This is all you have for me? This is all from your mission to the castle?'

Owen was with some difficulty staying cool and collected, his emotions having risen since the King's response. It was a sharp and disagreeable reminder of his own father, of punishment in the dark cell of a castle dungeon.

Expecting a fist applied to his ear, he bowed again. 'If Your Majesty will examine these coins, they are Spanish, from the reign of King Philip.'

Tam had recovered two of the coins and handed them to Owen. The third had rolled away inaccessible under the stone seat.

The King now examined the coins closely, turning them over eagerly as a light of hope was beginning to dawn, momentarily chasing away his gloomy feelings of anger and frustration.

Owen exchanged a glance with Marie and said more calmly than he felt, 'They are not only Spanish, sire, but from Fast Castle.'

A gleam of triumph appeared on the royal countenance as King James repeated, 'From Fast Castle, eh. Then we shall proceed there with further investigations.'

A small gesture indicated their dismissal. There

was no thanks, no mention of reward, not that Owen cared. He still had one opportunity not to be missed, to introduce Marie.

'May I present Lady Marie Hepburn, who is also Your Majesty's half-sister.' He gave an awkward smile. 'You have the same mother, sire.'

This was clearly no pleasant reminder for the King, who barely glanced at Marie deeply curtseying at Owen's side. He had little interest in young females at any time.

However, that young man beside her was a different matter. Handsome, aye, well-set-up.

The gesture of dismissal was for Owen and Marie, but not for Tam Eildor.

'You, lad. Bide with us a while. I would have your company.'

King James was attracted to him, as if linked by a gossamer thread. Neither fully remembered the extent of their previous meeting, when Tam had travelled to investigate the notorious Gowrie Conspiracy.

Finding himself alone apart from the discarded favourite and lingering courtiers, His Majesty was advancing towards him, smiling, the royal arms outstretched in a welcoming embrace. Tam retreated one step, having sensed his danger, and with little hope of rescue, he pressed the panic button.

There was a small whirring sound and the King, who had turned to dismiss his favourite and the courtiers, discovered that his outstretched hands had touched nothing. His prey had vanished.

* * *

Tam opened his eyes, grateful to have escaped King James' amorous intentions, but dismayed to find that he had not returned to his own time. What period had the panic button landed him in?

There were a lot of people. Newsboys shouted, 'Madeleine Smith trial!'

This must be 1857. He was amazed, overjoyed. The time machine had amended its mistake and sent him to his intended destination.

Bewildered he looked around, heartened to discover that he was in Edinburgh, leaning on a bench opposite the Court of Justice.

He was feeling a little dizzy and watched as people emerged from the court. They were well-dressed, opulent and very different to those he had left in 1587. The air was sweeter, too, and the street cobblestoned.

He stared around in confusion; his presence has attracted attention. An official of the law, a helmeted policeman, became interested in this stranger's unsteady manner. To say nothing of his clothes.

The policeman sighed. Another drunk for the jail? Keeping his truncheon close at hand, he approached and asked, 'Can I help you, sir?'

Nearness doesn't always bring the familiar and he was greeted with the unpleasant whiff of too much ale as the young man so oddly dressed looked round and asked, 'Er, the Madeleine Smith trial?'

He was not an Edinburgh lad, but that voice was educated.

Hmm. How interesting. The tall, young policeman

whose name – although it does not concern this chronicle – is Sergeant Jeremy Faro, regarded Tam sternly as he said: 'Am I in time, officer? I mean, for the trial?'

Was the stranger from Glasgow? No, more like the Highlands.

'Alas, no, sir.' The policeman indicated the people dispersing. 'It is over. You're too late. It ended a couple of hours ago.'

He was an odd sort of chap, this stranger. He wore old-fashioned clothes, a white shirt with drawstring neck and wide sleeves, tight leather breeches, thigh boots.

The policeman's curiosity was aroused. 'Come far, have you, sir?'

Tam sighs. 'Yes, a very long way. Is it July 9th?'

'It is.'

'Was the verdict not proven?'

'It was. The lady has already left Edinburgh by the back entrance, for safety.'

Across the crowded street, near St Giles, there was a scuffle, a pickpocket.

They both heard a shout of 'Stop thief!'

The policeman saluted Tam and began the chase.

Left alone, Tam considered what he has been told. The trial had ended and the verdict was not proven. He had arrived too late to meet her.

Too bad. He looked around. Despite the stiff breeze, it was a pleasant sunny day.

1587 was already a fading tapestry, dissolving. But 1857 was what he had intended, and Edinburgh looked good.

Newsboys were shouting the verdict.

He decided to buy a newspaper. Putting his hand in his pocket, the coin he recovered from under the stone seat in the arbour at Holyrood is still there. He looked at it and wondered who would want an old foreign coin, but he is hungry and this Spanish coin is pure gold. As such it should find a buyer and be worth a guinea maybe, enough for a comfortable short stay.

Tam straightened his shoulders. He would eat first, which should not be difficult as he sees several taverns, then find a place to lodge. From there he could decide on his next move.

1587 Orkney is lost.

1857 Edinburgh, an irresistible challenge, now exists.

ALANNA KNIGHT had more than seventy books published in an impressive writing career spanning over fifty years. She was a founding member and Honorary Vice President of the Scottish Association of Writers, Honorary President of the Edinburgh Writers' Club and member of the Scottish Chapter of the Crime Writers' Association. Alanna was awarded an MBE in 2014 for services to literature. Born and educated in Tyneside, she lived in Edinburgh until she passed away in 2020.